T0105656

Memories of the Heart

Beth Long

ISBN: 978-1-4269-6250-9 (sc)
ISBN: 978-1-4269-6249-3 (e)

Trafford rev. 04/07/2011

 www.trafford.com

North America & international
toll-free: 1 888 232 4444 (USA & Canada)
phone: 250 383 6864 ♦ fax: 812 355 4082

Contents

Thanks to my mother for her swift kick in the rear to get me going and to my three sisters who have always been my greatest fans. They have also given me much material throughout the years. I thank you daddy for always having a sense of humor. I miss you! A big thank you goes to my children for their computer skills, editing abilities, listening ears and happy spirits. Jim, I am most grateful to you for loving this wild and crazy girl. Lastly, thanks to Mr. Eichelman for telling me to use my talents and imagination.

Chapter 1

Blindsided

The icy cold numbness I felt had totally engulfed me. My heart was so heavy, just breathing took what small amount of energy I had inside. My body had the feeling of being frozen in time. Every one of my senses felt as if they had been switched off. There was a feeling of being dead inside. I moved without thinking and I thought without purpose. I was only going through the motions of living and feeling as if I were viewing myself from a distance.

Some well meaning people had told me that the numb, heavy feeling would go away. I hoped not. I didn't want to feel anything. One friend even told me that with time I would get over this. I could never get over losing my heart. I am sure someone, somewhere along the way told me that you can't live without your heart.

I couldn't imagine spending any time without David. For the past thirty-five years he had been a part of my life. David and my son, Michael, were my life. They were my reason for getting up each day. I had focused my last thirty-five years on caring for them and had enjoyed every moment. David would tell me everyday to do something for myself.

I always thought that I was doing for myself by being there for them. I have no regrets because I never thought I needed more than my family. When Michael married, David and I were alone again, just the two of us. We rediscovered that spending time together was what was most important. It was almost like being newlyweds, but with maturity and respect for each other that only comes with time.

Just three days before, David had kissed me goodbye, and twenty minutes later he was gone. My life changed in an instant. One minute I was married to the love of my life and the next minute I was his widow. He was such a wonderful driver, I trusted him completely. He had always taken great care of his family. How could he lose control of his car? How could he take his eyes off the road for even one second? How could he leave me? I didn't want to do this alone but I was alone for the rest of my life. The fear of living without David was completely paralyzing. I was angry and I was hurt. I was mad at David for dying and furious with God for taking David from me. My sadness was fueled by my anger. I wanted to awaken from this horrible dream but it wasn't a dream.

David's funeral came and went and I didn't remember any of it. I don't think that I cried because I'm sure that I used every tear the days before. I do remember how adorable my grandson looked in his suit. What a silly thing to remember at your husband's funeral.

I didn't even have enough energy to get out of that ugly black dress. I didn't ever want to wear black again. It's an awful reminder of David's death. Black is such a sad, forlorn color. Maybe it is the absence of color that makes it void of life. The dress didn't look particularly good on me, but it fit my grief. It looked like a garbage bag drooping from my shoulders. When I finally took it off, I threw it in the trash where it belonged, walked away and wished I could do that with my grief.

I wanted to sit in my bedroom forever. That was where I was sitting when the State Police called me. I had just finished making the bed and folding David's pajamas when the phone rang. I kept telling them they had the wrong Mrs. David Fry. Over and over I told them there must be some mistake. By the time I arrived at the hospital David had died. I wouldn't believe that my strong dear husband was gone. It literally took my breath away, and I think I didn't breathe for the rest of that day and for many days there after. Everything I did was like moving in slow motion.

I don't remember much of anything that took place for days and even weeks after the day David died. Time came and went and I went through the motions but that was all I did. Thank goodness for my brother, Joe. He took over and made all the arrangements for everything that followed. David had always wanted to make pre-funeral arrangements, but I just found it too morbid and couldn't bring myself to do that daunting task. I really thought I would die first. I never wanted to think about David and me not being together. I knew that I was never going to be able to let him go.

David would have handled this much better than I. All of the single women in town would have seen to it. Maybe even some of the married women. He was so handsome. Women would always look at him when he entered a room. David's tall, dark presence always caught their eye. Some women even flirted with him. I used to watch them when they weren't aware I was noticing and some didn't care if I did notice. David was very modest and he didn't pay them any attention. Maybe he really did, but he never let on to me. David made me feel very secure in our marriage and I always knew I was the only one for him. The little things that he did made me feel special. When we were out, David would always come up behind me and put his arms around me and kiss my cheek. I think he was just comforting me by showing his love outwardly and telling everyone that he loved me, Hannah Devon Fry. Oh how I love that name.

David was a wonderful Christian man. He was full of life and love. David was always helping strays, both people and animals. Once he invited a family he had met through and outreach program to Easter dinner. They had lost their home in a fire and he couldn't imagine the three children going without a good meal and a basket full of candy. That Easter was hectic but memorable. We had children running everywhere. David loved every minute of it and so did I. Our house was so full of laughter. David served on many charity boards and gave a donation to almost every person that asked. He had a special soft spot for the poor. If he had a fault, it was his inability to say no.

In the back of my mind I was thinking everyone would be better off if I had crashed. I thought my identity was because of David. People only knew me as David Fry's wife. What good could I be without him? I couldn't function with a broken heart. I felt like part of me was gone. Half of a person was what I had become. I had no energy and the only place I could go was to bed. Just to crawl in and pull the covers over my head and never come out was the only desire that I had at that time. I would have rather been dead than without David. I knew that God didn't want me; he never did. What had I ever done for anyone? He only wants people like David. I was brought up to believe that God was only a God for really good people and I didn't think of myself as a God-like person.

After the funeral, my son Michael came to the bedroom door and jolted me from my thoughts. "Mom! Reverend

Doss is here. Mom! Are you asleep?" Michael kept calling out to me.

"I can hear you Michael, but I'm not up to talking with anyone, and I really don't want to talk with him." I said fighting back the tears.

I remember him saying, "Mom, everyone means well. Reverend Doss is here for support. Dad would have never wanted you to shut everyone out and do this alone." Michael sounded so much like his father. He looked a lot like me but he was his father's child. He had such a reasonable tone about him and calmness that mimicked his father's demeanor.

"Oh, really? Then, why did he leave me? Why did he leave me alone to do all of this?" I sobbed. Anger and grief had taken me completely over. I didn't feel strong and didn't care. My strength had come from David. He was my rock.

"Mom, I have to believe that God needed Dad. I don't understand any of this…but I have to trust that God needs Dad. We will see him when our time on this earth is over. Don't shut Him out. Dad would be so… never mind mom. I'll tell Reverend Doss you will call him later when you are feeling better," Michael said as he walked away from the door. That was his belief, not mine. I thought God was incredibly selfish. What God had done for me is left me alone and taken away my soul.

I called out to Michael and asked him to come back and sit with me for a while. All I wanted to do was tell him over and over how much I loved him, and I knew his father loved him with all of his heart. I just needed Michael to sit for a while with me before he had to go home to his family. I was afraid that I would lose him too and I just wanted him close to me.

Michael soon returned after telling his wife, Mary Lee, to take the children home. They had been there all day and were getting restless. Michael and Mary Lee had been married for eight years and had three precious children. Their life together was almost picture perfect or as perfect as a marriage could be with three children and the stresses of real life. Mary Lee was such a support to Michael during this sad time. Heaven knows he needed support. They both were my strength, and I needed them so very much.

Michael came back upstairs and sat with me for hours. We talked about everything. I told him how proud I was of his accomplishments in work and especially what a great father and husband he had grown to be. We talked about how he had married the perfect life partner. I think that they are as devoted to each other as David and I were. In some ways, maybe that wasn't a good thing. How hard it is for the one left to go on without the other.

I think I was really afraid to let David go because I was afraid I would forget him, and I didn't want that to ever happen. All I had left were my memories.

Michael left only because I insisted he go home. My little brother Joe, had wanted to stay with me, but I really didn't want anyone around. I felt like a burden and I just wanted to be alone in the silence. There I was in the house for the first time without David I hadn't been home since the day he died. I had been at Michael's and surrounded by my family. I was alone with only my thoughts and my memories. As I cried myself to sleep, I thought about what would I do with the rest of my life? Who would hold me when I was lost? Who would warm my feet when they were chilled by winter's breath? With whom would I share my day or who would tell me about his day? The changes were so overwhelming and I was suffocating.

It wasn't supposed to be like this. We were going to grow old together and walk off into the sunset hand in hand. As

I cried, I wished for David over and over. I went from anger to hurt in a matter of seconds.

Michael said God would help me through this, but where was He? How could God help? He had taken my life from me. All I could feel at that moment was anger and hate for God. He wasn't my God. The God I would choose would not be a God of destruction.

"Who is Hannah Devon Fry?"

Chapter 2

One Week Later

I wished the phone would stop ringing. I would have rather gotten cards from people and not phone calls. All I could do was cry when they called. It just kept reminding me of how much I missed David. They were well meaning, but annoying.

Michael was coming by to take me to the bank. I didn't want to deal with any of that, but Michael said that we needed to do it as soon as possible and now was the time. I hated the thought of finances. David had always taken care of everything. He understood all the language and financial talk. I had to laugh because I knew that if David were watching me, he would be laughing because he knew how intimidated I was. He had always tried to teach me a few things, but I managed to find a way to change the subject. I had no brain for business.

Michael had assured me that I had nothing to worry about because David had left me financially comfortable. Whatever did that mean? I had no needs or wants now that David was gone. I only had Michael, Mary Lee, and my three precious grand children, Lyle, Sissy, and Sarah. I had thought that I would be better off giving them everything and Michael could just give me an allowance. I only wanted things to be easier because everything was overwhelming me. I decided to tell Mr. Price, the banker, my idea and hoped that Michael would agree. I really didn't want to fool with anything, especially money and finances. What I really wanted was for David to walk through the door and tell me I had just had a bad dream. I knew that was not going to happen but I still thought about it more often than not.

When Michael got there, he was full of energy and ready to get things done. I couldn't imagine having that kind of energy. Everything I did had so much effort behind it. I really didn't think all this was necessary at that time and I could have prolonged it forever.

On the way to the bank, Michael kept telling me Reverend Doss wanted to come by to see me. I just sat there listening. I guess I really didn't care one way or the other. It wasn't going to change things. Maybe I was showing some progress or at least moving in the right direction. Maybe I was inching back into the real world again. Just a week ago, I wanted the Reverend to leave me alone and let me cry by myself.

When we arrived at the bank, Mr. Price greeted me with a somber tone. I almost laughed because everyone I had talked to since David's death used the same somber, almost morbid tone. The only people that talk to me in a normal voice are Michael and the children. In fact, Michael almost talks to me as if nothing happened. I hadn't thought about that until that very moment. That was exactly the way David talked to me when my father died. He was very businesslike and very matter of fact. I guessed it was their way of helping me get through my grief and not thinking about their own feelings. I kept thinking at any time Michael was going to look at me and say "Buck up, mom."

Mr. Price told me how sorry he was for my loss and then went right into telling me about all of these investments that David had made. When he paused, I told Mr. Price and Michael about my idea of giving everything to Michael and just giving me an allowance. Michael about fell over and told me how silly I was. Mr. Price said that wouldn't be necessary because it could be set up in a trust and they could automatically deposit money into my account. Michael said to leave the money the way David had intended it to be distributed. He thought if his father had wanted it that way, then we should leave it alone. Michael and Mr. Price got all the documents together and I seemed to sign papers until my hands ached. I didn't pay attention to what I was signing. I just signed Hannah Devon Fry, Hannah Devon Fry, Hannah Devon Fry over and over and over again until my hand about fell off. At this point, I had about grown tired of my own name.

Michael said there would be plenty of money in my account to take care of all my bills. What bills would I have? The house was paid off and David paid for my car when he bought it for my birthday last year. How much money could I possibly need?

Mr. Price asked me if I knew that David had left a sizable sum to the Church. I told him I didn't know this but his generosity never ceased to surprise me. He, also, set up an endowed scholarship to the Virginia Military Institute. He was a 1966 graduate of VMI. I wasn't at all shocked by that. David was so proud of his connection to such a school steeped in history and tradition. The Institute boasted of many famous men who had passed through the arches. Men of military history had been a part of the same school from which David had graduated. General George Marshall, General Ramsey Clark, and even Stonewall Jackson had passed through the stone arches.

David and I started dating while he was attending VMI. I would go to Lexington for football games and dances just to be with him. Girls would stay in town at various homes. I always stayed at a home owned by Mrs. Livingston. She was a widow and would open her house to young ladies for date weekends. Times have certainly changed. Forty years ago, it was unheard of for girls to stay in a hotel or with their date. I thought that the Keydets looked so handsome in their uniforms. David was quite proud of that uniform.

Once, while visiting VMI, when Michael was very small, he asked David if he had lived in that castle. David laughed and told him he had lived there for four years, but no one ever called it a castle. The Institute stood like a fortress that could withstand the stresses of all time.

Many of David's friends had been able, over the past few years, to give some money in various ways to VMI. Some of the brother rats, which they are called, gave to the athletic departments while others chose to give to the foundation. He had always wanted to do something that would make a real difference in someone's life. He felt that he had received so much from the school. David thought of VMI as a way of life not just a place to receive an education. He was strongly convinced that it was a character building experience. He beamed with pride every time he talked about his school.

David always saw the good in people, and I don't think that came from his schooling but it was just his trusting nature. I always felt he was a little naïve, so I made up for his lack of suspicion. David and I were so different. I guess that is why we complimented each other. Opposites do attract.

I could see in Michael's face that he was so proud of his generous father. Michael wasn't able to go to VMI because of a heart problem discovered at birth. He would have loved to have followed in his father's footsteps.

Michael had a valve problem and still has to have his heart checked. Once a year, he goes through a whole regime of tests. His son, Lyle, had the same problem, but the doctor's fixed it while Mary Lee was pregnant. Mary Lee took it all in stride. I guess being a nurse made it a lot easier on her. She understood the procedure. She stayed optimistic through it all and Lyle is a healthy boy.

While Michael was young I hovered over Michael like a mother hen. David was so afraid I would make him a weak, timid child. Luckily that never happened because Michael turned out to be such a strong individual.

I must have been a million miles away because when Mr. Price asked me if I understood everything, I almost jumped out of my chair because my mind was somewhere else. I told him everything was fine if Michael approved. Michael nodded in agreement.

Michael thanked Mr. Price for everything he had done and told him how comfortable we were in knowing that my finances were in such capable hands. I wondered how Michael had such confidence in someone he had just met. There's my suspicious nature I thought to myself. Michael amazed me at how similar he and his father were.

On the way home, Michael asked me to come home with him and spend some time with my grandchildren. Lyle and Sissy would be coming home from school and Sarah should be up from her nap. I really didn't want to go, but Michael insisted. I guess that was just what I needed because, for a brief time, I didn't think of my loneliness. The voices of the children made me feel as if nothing had changed, almost as if time had stopped. I needed this distraction and somehow Michael knew just what to do. I had wrapped myself in a shroud of grief and could see nothing else. Slowly, I was beginning to peel away bits and pieces, but I was unaware of the process. With each smile or laugh from the children, my shroud began to loosen her wrapping around my heart.

When I came home that night, I wrote in my journal. I was beginning to feel again. These emotions were up and down, but I thought that writing about them maybe would help me somehow get through. I picked up my pencil and wrote until I was so sleepy I drifted off into a deep, dreamless sleep.

"What would I do without my family?"

Chapter 3

One Month Later

It was getting close to Thanksgiving. The air had a chill even though the sun was warm. This was David's favorite time of the year. He loved to play golf. Anytime he could sneak away for eighteen holes he would, that's where David seemed the happiest. When he had a golf club in his hand and felt the fresh, crisp, green grass under his feet, it appeared as though he forgot business and every other stress in his life. I never understood his passion for golf, but I enjoyed knowing that he was doing something that he truly loved. I look back now and wish that I had shared his love of golf. I always acted like I was listening to him when he would come home and give me a shot by shot playback of all eighteen holes. Now, I wish he would walk through the door and I would listen to every word. He, probably, felt that way about my tennis; even though I never had the same love for tennis that David had for golf.

I hadn't played tennis in since David's death. I really didn't want to go hear all those people talk in their somber tones about my loss. Besides, they really didn't care. Until it touches you personally, you don't understand. Some of the girls I played with have checked in but I haven't seen them since the funeral. It was, probably, not their fault but mine because I kept to myself and avoided acquaintances. Oh, I knew people are at a loss for words, so they chose not to say anything. It's such an awkward situation and most people choose not to put themselves there.

There were no words that anyone could use to make me feel better. I couldn't feel better. I just didn't feel as badly as I did the day before. I knew that I wasn't the first woman to lose her husband, but at that time, I was the only one that mattered. Yes, I'm selfish! I knew that I was feeling sorry for myself but, when I started to feel better I almost felt guilty.

I went to Michaels often to help take my mind off myself. The children were really the light of my life. When I would go home to my empty house, the guilt of feeling better overwhelmed me. I still didn't understand why David died and I was still here. I was really afraid to have fun again. I was afraid that I would forget that I had lost David. Maybe, I was truly afraid that I would forget who David was and what he had meant to me. Deep down, I knew that was not possible. I missed not sharing everything with him. I miss his smile but most of all I miss his hugs.

Oh my, it hurts. We planned a wonderful future together. He was thinking about retiring in a few years. We talked about moving to Pinehurst, North Carolina. He always called it the golf Mecca of the South. One anniversary, we stayed at one of the beautiful inns. The lobby of the hotel was so warm and inviting and off to the left was a beautiful mahogany bar shipped in from England that caught his eye. The entire room was so masculine. David just fell in love with the décor. I truly think he would have loved it if our house looked just like that inn. I just continued to use pastels and florals. Now, I would live in a gym if he would just come back. David never complained, he was always complimenting my taste and my sense of design. Occasionally, he would make a suggestion but I never paid any attention. I regret that.

I still hadn't gotten up enough strength to go through David's things. Michael had offered to help, but I really couldn't bear to do this emotionally draining task. I just thought that if I got rid of his things, it was admitting that David was gone forever. I couldn't think about that. I still wished I could wake up from that horrible dream. I missed him more and it's wasn't getting any easier. I cried less but maybe because I had no more tears to cry.

As I sat there I heard the doorbell ring. I thought that if I pretended I wasn't home whoever it was would go away. I thought it could be Michael but he couldn't get in because I had been putting the deadbolt on the door. I used to never do that. I seemed to have an uneasy feeling all the time. I never had been afraid before all of this but I just felt as if my heart would beat out of my throat since David's death. The doctor had given me something for anxiety but I hadn't used it. I didn't like the way I felt. I didn't want to feel what I was feeling but I didn't want to be in a fog either.

The doorbell rang again. I ran down the stairs. I wished David had put the peep hole in the front door. He must have been going to do that because there sat the peep hole and the drill on the table beside the front door. I'm sure that he was planning to get to that when he came home but he never came home.

I took a deep breath, after running down the stairs, and quickly opened the door. I was expecting to see Michael standing there, but instead there was Reverend Doss. He was grinning from ear to ear. I guess he was so pleased to see that I was home and finally had opportunity to tell me about his Jesus gobblety goop. I was, totally, unable to speak.

Very politely he asked if this was a bad time. How could I tell the preacher that anytime was bad for me? He commented on how busy I looked. I think back on that and I bet I was a real sight. Maybe even a little frightening.

I realized I hadn't invited him in and apologized. Where were my manners? I guessed I lost my manners along with everything else the day David died.

I really did not want to talk about the past few weeks but I knew that was exactly why he was there to see me. I thought I knew all the things that he would say. I wanted him to tell me life wasn't fair and God should have never done this to me. Of course he didn't. He told me I needed to be in church along with my church family. He said that I was greatly missed in choir. I wanted to tell him the only reason I ever sung in the choir was because David and Michael wanted me to. David always told me I had a God given talent and I should not waste it. David was the one who got up on Sundays and fixed breakfast so I would get up and get moving in order that we make it on time. He always hated to be late because he and Michael sat on the front row so that they could see me sing. I couldn't imagine singing again and not being able to see David Smiling at me. I couldn't think of being able to sing to the glory of God when I wasn't feeling His grace. God took my David away!

When Michael was a teenager he would want to sleep in some Sundays but David always told him if he could have fun on Saturday nights he could get up for church. I tried to talk him into letting us sleep in all the time but he never gave in. Michael has such a strong church background and I give all the credit to his father. Michael and Mary Lee are very active in church. He will be just as strict as his father. The apple really doesn't fall far from the tree. The church is a big part of their family life.

I never told anyone how I felt about church because I knew how important it was for us to be there as a family. It would have hurt David for me to tell him. Thus, I never said a word.

It's not that I hated God. I really didn't hate Him. I just didn't understand his ways. Why someone as good as my father and David died and my mother and I are still here boggled my mind. My mother and I weren't exactly great Christian women.

My mother and I weren't close. She always preferred my brother, Joe. That was alright by me because my father and David were my biggest fan. The two loves of my life are gone.

I looked at Rev. Doss and asked him why I should come back.

He was floored at my bluntness. Very quickly he replied, "When we are in need, we should be with our family and the church. That is all the family anyone needs." He then told me that the church needed me. I couldn't fathom why he would think that.

I told him that I would think about it but he kept coming at me with reasons why I should be there. He was right about one thing; He said, "You must be lonely." Wow! He was so right. I knew I needed something, but I wasn't sure just what that could was.

He stayed over an hour. We had coffee and talked about everything. The visit that I had dreaded so much turned out to be quite pleasant. He offered his wife to help me go through David's things if I needed her to. He insisted she was a great purger.

I was growing extremely tired and it must have shown in my face because he jumped up and said he had been there too long and needed to be home soon. I thanked him for everything' and told him I needed to go through David's personal belongings myself.

I knew that I would get a strong sense of him just by touching his things and smelling his scent. Reverend Doss asked a prayer before he left. I didn't hear the words but I did feel some comfort in knowing someone prayed for me.

I watched him walk away and I was jealous of his wife. Her husband was coming home to her. I thought… what a lucky woman.

"My God, my God, why have you forsaken me?"
- Matthew 27:46

Chapter 4

January

Thanksgiving and Christmas have come and gone. I thought that they would never come. Once they came, I blinked and they were gone. I was happy to just get through them without any major breakdown. I did go to Christmas Eve service with Michael and his family. It was a beautiful service but so very hard for me to sit through. It felt strange not having David with us.

Lyle, my oldest grandchild, sang a solo and the girls were dressed as angels. Lyle has a pretty voice that belongs in the heavens. Mary Lee tells anyone and everyone who listens, that he inherited it from his grandmother. Of course, that pleases me to no end.

Lyle had made me a Christmas card that said he loved me and hoped that I wouldn't be sad forever. He signed it, "Your Grandson, Lyle." I guessed he thought I wouldn't know who he was. It touched my heart that he made it for me. I still have all the cards that Michael made me through the years. I hugged Lyle and told him I wouldn't be sad forever, but I didn't have a clue whether that was true or not. It was too soon to tell.

Was I lying to him? I hoped not, but at that time I was so alone in my thoughts. There were still times that I felt as if I was in a vacuum or maybe a hole that I couldn't get out of. How long was I going to feel this way? I knew a woman, years ago, who grieved so long that she started believing that her husband was alive. I would often see her carrying on conversations with nothing but the air. I guess she just lost touch with reality. It was so sad but she seemed happy again.

January is one of those months that makes me feel down. Everything is brown outside. Christmas is over and all the decorations are put away. The first Christmas without David, I only put a wreath on the door. The worst thing about it, it was artificial. At that time, that's about how I felt, artificial. I would have never used anything but real greenery in the past. I guess that everything changed in a single heartbeat. Nothing was the same.

I don't remember much about those past few weeks. I was hoping that time wouldn't erase all of my memories. Some of the people told me when David died that time would heal my broken heart. I think that time only helps your pain lessen but it never completely goes away. One thing that time can't do is take away my loneliness. It just gets greater. You can try to feel the void with meaningless tasks, but loneliness always creeps back into your heart.

I still needed to go through David's things. I think that, finally, I was feeling ready. I had no idea that it would be one of the hardest things I've ever done in my life. I just needed to take my time and savor every moment with what was left of my sweet love.

I really knew that Michael wanted to help. I kept forgetting that he was hurting too. He had handled his sadness very differently from me. He had his children, his wife and his work to keep him busy. I think that keeping busy was the answer, but, I just didn't have the energy.

The first thing that Michael would try to do was remove his father's old sweater from the back of the chair in the bedroom. That would be the last thing that I would want to remove because it still smells of David's cologne. I hold it sometimes just to feel him close to me. I think that if I can't have him next to me, I could at least imagine him in my heart.

Sometimes when I hold it, I remember dancing with David. He was a marvelous dancer. David loved to dance slowly. He hated fast dancing but always loved beach music and shagging. He had a wonderful sense of rhythm and seemed to glide across the floor like air. He also, loved to play the guitar and had wanted to take piano lessons. David was a closet musician, only playing for him and me. He would play old vinyl records of Faranti and Teicher while closing his eyes and losing himself in their sound.

On our tenth anniversary, we went to the gorgeous mountains located in Blowing Rock, North Carolina. The mountains were so beautiful. I still can picture how they seemed to wrap you in their majesty. Michael was a tiny baby and David had made arrangements for a babysitter and had set everything in motion. I had no idea what he had planned, but I never knew what was up his sleeve. I just recognized his wry smile and knew he was planning something.

When we arrived at the cabin and I opened the door, there sat a wonderful picnic in front of a roaring fire. He had bought a beautiful handmade quilt which he had placed meticulously on the floor with our picnic laid upon its intricate stitches. He must have had the quilt made for me because it was in all my favorite colors and he knew I had wanted a pink and green quilt for the guest room. I was totally in shock. I just began to cry. David was so afraid that I didn't like what he had done for me, but I finally convinced him I was crying because he had made me so happy. David always made me feel special. A man like David is so rare.

That night, we danced for hours and never seemed to tire. I remembered everything as if it had just happened. We didn't have a lot of money; but who needs money when someone loves you that much?

As I woke from my thoughts, I realized that I had been daydreaming in my closet for hours and was still faced with a closet full of his things. David would never leave my thoughts. No matter how hard I tried to move forward. How could this be all that was left of the man that I loved for over thirty-five years? The things were still there but David was gone.

Night always seemed to come so quickly and silently. Here I sat on the floor of my closet in the darkness. It got dark so quickly in January. Soon winter's chill would slowly be leaving to make way for summer's warmth. I love the summer. I couldn't wait to be outside more. I knew that it would help with my sadness to be in the warm sunshine. I didn't think I was depressed but I just had a sense of loss. Something was missing from my life. I knew what was missing and I could do nothing about it.

Slowly and very methodically I went through David's things. I started small, a belt, a pair of socks and an old pair of athletic shoes. Then I found an old bedroom shoe under the cabinet. David swore I had thrown it away to keep him from wearing them. I laughed because he never believed me when I would tell him that I didn't throw it away, but confessed I was glad it was gone. The bedroom shoes looked like "old man" shoes. I always called them "shuffle" shoes. You know the kind of shoes you see old men wearing, shuffling to the paper box to get the morning paper. David insisted that they were the most comfortable shoes he had ever owned.

After a couple of hours of going through David's things, I was totally exhausted. It wasn't quite as bad of a task as I thought it would be. Maybe the timing was right or maybe celebrating our past was good for my soul. I had packed up four boxes of well organized treasures. I could only imagine what I was going to do with them.

I crawled into bed for the first time in months feeling as if I was moving forward. I had been standing still for months just waiting for David to come home to me. I guess, finally, I was coming to the realization he was never coming home again.

"Sad but true, numb but alive"

Chapter 5

Soul Warming

Spring was peeking out from behind the clouds. It took the months of February and March to go through and clean out David's belongings. I not only disposed of many of his things but I also took the opportunity to go through mine. Day by day, I went through his clothes. I even had the energy to go to the office and look through the boxes that Michael had so neatly packed. Michael had gone through what he needed for business and had tucked away David's personal items in unused paper boxes. Michael must have done this shortly after David's death because the boxes had begun to gather dust. There wasn't much to throw away because David was a man of extreme organization. There were no t's left to cross and no I's that need to be dotted. He had even ordered my birthday present from Tiffany's. I looked forward to always opening my little blue box each birthday. He usually gave me a charm or a cloisonné egg for my bracelets. There was no card but I was sure he would have bought it at least a month before my birthday. He loved to shop for the perfect card. I think of cards as a bit of a waste which is hard to believe because I saved every card

Michael and David gave me. My birthday wasn't even until March. That was so like David, well prepared. If Michael had known that the box was there he would have given it to me on my birthday. He must have just gathered things and not thought about what he was doing. That sounds familiar. I opened the box fully expecting a charm and there was a beautiful, solid gold, dome ring. I had looked at it for years, but thought it was silly to want such a luxury. I really only wore my engagement ring and wedding band. I put the over extravagant dome ring on my finger and it fit perfectly. I felt at that moment he was with me. I imagined how proud of himself he would have been. Not because of the ring, but how he had been so sly in surprising me.

When I had gotten home, I got a cup of tea, sat at the secretary, and then I wrote again in my journal. "I'm feeling much better. I still have an enormous void in my life, but somehow I get through the days without so many tears though I still cry."

Purpose, that's a word that keeps coming to mind. I had never thought of that before in my life. When I was young my purpose was to go to school, be a good girl and find the right husband. That was exactly what I did. I was the adoring wife and the loving mother I was supposed to be. What more could a girl want? I never felt that I needed or wanted anything else."

The warmer April days had been beckoning me to get outside. I loved walking in my yard. Everywhere I looked small signs of spring were all around. The May Apples just were starting to peak their unopened umbrella shapes through the mulch. Soon they would be opened and their white flowers blooming.

David loved that part of the yard. He had built a frame for his hammock. As you would walk through the Arbor into the backyard, you would immediately want to go to the hammock. Many times when he would work in the yard, he would disappear after an hour. I always knew where to look. He would be there relaxing. Many times I would join him and we would dream about our travels when he retired. David didn't have the word "hurry" in his vocabulary. Though very efficient, he never rushed through life. Mowing the lawn always took most of the day. He was constantly trying to get me to learn how but I never would take hold of the handles and try. If the truth be known I thought mowing was hard work and I hated to sweat. I loved my flowers but lawn mowers have a sharp blade and I am not the most coordinated person.

Mowing the lawn was another thing that would need to be done. Now I had to learn to mow and sweat. I was scared to death to try but someone had to get the job done. I wanted to ask Michael but I knew he is so busy with his own yard and family. I had the bright idea that he could show me how and I would do it myself. I didn't really have a hobby, so, I thought maybe yard work could be just that time filler that I was looking for. I needed something that would exhaust me enough to stay asleep. In the past, I never had trouble falling asleep, but after David died, I couldn't stay asleep. I would wake up feeling as if I had been run over by a truck. I had a reoccurring dream that I was looking for something and couldn't find it. I never knew what I was looking for and I would awaken before I could find whatever it was. Though, I knew, within my heart of hearts, just what or who I was trying to find.

Hopefully, I thought I would have a few more weeks before the lawn needed to be mown. Many times in April, snow had fallen in Virginia, just when you thought that spring was there to stay.

The house across the street went on the market that afternoon. The couple was moving to Florida. Mr. and

Mrs. Adams had been married for sixty years. They were so cute together. When they walked in the afternoons they always held hands. I would picture David and I walking and holding hands. There were times I even felt his hand in mine. I was a little jealous at times. Then I would think about the fact that they ate at four o'clock and went to bed at seven. Now that, extinguished my jealousy. I would have done anything to have David back here with me, but I didn't think that we would ever go to be at seven o'clock or even go to an early bird special for those ten percent discount meals. David enjoyed coming in and reading the paper, sharing a glass of wine and eating around seven. Like I said, he never was in a great hurry.

I watched television until the wee hours of the morning. Some mornings I slept until ten. I would stay up watching television just for the noise. I guess it kept me company. I knew every slice and dice machine that was ever manufactured. I even got engrossed in an infomercial about a meat slicer. It would slice twenty pounds of meat at a time. Why would anyone need that much sliced meat?

The phone rang me back to my senses. I often caught myself not focusing on anything. At the time I had such a small attention span, though I was unaware. If I would focus on the present, I would find myself feeling very lonely. I chose to think of the past when David and I were together. My memories seem to fill a void. If only for a while, I would forget my heavy heart.

Michael was on the phone. He made some small talk. He really just wanted to check on me. I couldn't wait to tell him my idea about mowing the lawn. I think I really wanted him to tell me he would get someone to do it but he didn't. He thought it would be a great thing for me to learn how. I learned that Mary Lee had been mowing their lawn for years. I wondered how she fit everything into her busy schedule. I was almost speechless but I told him I would try. He told me he would never turn me out to pasture unless he thought I could handle it. I laughed, but didn't think that I would be very good at mowing or sweating.

I decided and hoped that I could learn anything if I put my mind to it. This was a real change in my attitude. I was feeling a little more independent. Everyday, I discovered something that I didn't know how to do. I had never changed the battery in the smoke alarm. When it started to beep, I had to figure it out on my own because I couldn't find Michael or Mary Lee. After a while, I got the cover off and replaced the battery. Somehow, try as I might, I couldn't get the smoke alarm back together. I truly think that baking a seven layer cake was easier than changing the battery. The cover just hung there until Michael came to my rescue and replaced it.

There still were moments that I was so angry with David for leaving me alone. I felt, overwhelmingly, helpless at times. I had to learn so many new things because I was on my own. I had to face the fact I was a widow. That word would make me cringe. I preferred the catch phrase W.O.T.O. (women on their own). I wished everyday that I could turn back the clock. I would have been happy to have had one more day with David, one more kiss, one more hug. It's wasn't fair. My daddy used to tell me life wasn't fair, it was just life. That was really prophetic. Now, at fifty-something, I am experiencing his words as truth.

"To mow or not to mow? That is the question."

Chapter 6

June - Summer's Finally Here

I had learned how to start the mower. I had even used the weed eater. I wasn't very good at either but I couldn't see hiring someone to do it when I really was capable. I could tell that Michael didn't think the yard looked very good but he never said a word. He only made a sour face. As if he had stepped in doggie doo. I knew that yard work would not be my hobby. Not only was I not very good at it but I really didn't like to get hot and sweaty.

The house across the street sold. I didn't ever see anyone looking at it but they were getting ready to move in. The Adams moved about a week ago. I will miss them so much. I loved watching them and loved seeing their devotion to each other. The new homeowners have some big shoes to fill.

David had been gone for eight months. I would fill my days as much as I could with menial tasks. The nights were the loneliest time. They seemed so long. I ached to have him hold me again. I missed that part of our life most of all. It wasn't even about the sexual part of marriage, it was about the intimacy. It was mostly about the quiet "I love you's" after making love. It is the total feeling of being held by someone who knows you from within. It was about the someone who would breathe in sync with you as if you were one. I missed most of all his big hand holding mine.

I couldn't imagine anything worse than loneliness. It had only been eight months for me. Some choose a life of loneliness and some are catapulted into that life style. I was there, not by choice, but none the less, without David. I hated the fact that I couldn't change any of this. I would find myself trying to bargain with God. I would beg Him to bring David back to me. Then I would get angry with God. I slammed doors and even threw a glass once. I just felt out of control. Once I would regain some sense about me, I would feel guilty for yelling at God.

I was finding myself talking to God more and more. There were times I talked and times I yelled. I always blamed Him for what happened or maybe I blamed Him for not preventing what had happened. I would tell God how much I hated Him though I knew that I didn't. That would make Michael so very mad. He would always tell me that God did nothing to me but could do a lot for me. Michael would continually tell how much God needed David in Heaven but I wondered if God knew how much I needed David with me.

I did promise Michael that I would attend church more often. I found that promise hard to keep but a promise was just that, a promise. I knew that it wouldn't hurt but I really didn't think it could help as much as Michael thought.

Reverend Doss still came by to see me. He does understand my grief. His son died at a very young age. He said that his wife took a long time healing. I couldn't imagine how anyone could heal from the loss of a child. I would almost feel guilty when he would console me. He had an incredible strength. I was guessing it came from that "God thing" he talked about.

David had that "God thing." He trusted God and always put things in God's hands. He always told me God had big shoulders and he could carry all of our problems. His parents had "it" and Michael has "it."

Now my father was a good man but not particularly religious. My mother wasn't religious at all and drank far too much and far too often to have that "God thing." If you talked to my brother Joe he would only tell you she was a social drinker but everyone knew better. He just couldn't admit that she was an alcoholic. After our dad's death, she moved in with Joe and his wife.

Joe called me a lot after David's death but my mother never called. If I would call over there she would never answer the phone because she could see on the caller I.D. and wouldn't answer if she saw my name.

Louise Devon had never forgiven me for trying to get dad to leave her and take us with him when I was twelve years old. She never loved him and talked to him with such disdain. I think she was so angry with him because he never made her rich. She wanted to be high society, but would have never fit in. My mother wasn't a happy woman. She never smiled unless she was insulting someone. She seemed to gain great pleasure in other's misery.

My dad owned a shoe repair shop, Marty Devon's Shoe repair. Everyone loved him. He would fix anyone's shoes whether they could pay him or not. He would write a receipt and put it into the register drawer. He never thought about it again. Sometimes he would get paid but most of the time he didn't.

When daddy died we found hundreds of receipts. My mother wanted us to hunt "deadbeats" down for payment. Joe and I knew most of the people were dead or had moved away. We would have never pursued them any way. My dad was a generous man and wanted to help people out anyway that he could. Fixing their shoes was a simple thing, but to him it was the right thing to do.

Joe even agreed with me and told mother that it would be impossible. She was mad at him for weeks. She needed Joe so she couldn't stay mad for long, just until the next drink.

We knew daddy would never want us to look for those people so we agreed not to do anything. Joe put them away in a box. I didn't know then why he didn't burn them but he just couldn't let them go.

My mother was always mad about something I would or wouldn't do. One of those times was when I wanted to go to college. She thought that college was unnecessary for girls. She really was from the thinking that women should stay home and be supported by their husbands. She never worked outside the house and thought I shouldn't waste time or money on college. Though she never worked she wanted me to work as soon as it was legal. So I began working at fifteen as a waitress at a little greasy spoon, Frank's Fish Fry.

Throughout my life I had felt invisible. It wasn't until I met David, that someone found me interesting. How could I not fall in love with him? When I was in school I was never the best in math class and I didn't write that perfect essay. I did sing in the school choir. Mr. Taub, the director, was always complimenting my voice but every time a solo was available, Paige Moore would be picked. Of course, she was beautiful and had a nice voice. Paige was Miss Everything. She was a cheerleader, prom queen, and number one in our class. The worst part of it all was she was the nicest person you would ever want to meet. I wanted to hate her, but I couldn't. Finally when I went to college I had many solos. Maybe it was because I had lost my adolescent awkwardness.

Dating was new to me so when I met David, I fell hard. He loved me and yes, I fell for my first love. I was certainly in the right place at the right time. If I had listened to my mother I would have never met David. That didn't matter to my mother because she only saw things her way.

She really resented the fact that I only went to Roanoke College for three years and never graduated. I had wasted time and money in her eyes. Repeatedly, she told me I had proven her point about women going to college. When I met David he wanted to get married as soon as he graduated from VMI. He was afraid that he would have to go the Vietnam and we would never get married. So I dropped out of school with intentions of going back but I never did. David wouldn't have cared if I had wanted to back but I never did. Mother wasn't happy about any of those decisions. Louise let it be known to the world when she wasn't happy and that was most of the time.

"Does the apple fall far from the tree?"

Chapter 7
Life Goes On

Summer arrived with a vengeance. It was ninety degrees at nine o'clock in the morning. What flowers hadn't been overcome by the heat looked as if they melting. I can remember when my father would say it was hot enough to fry an egg on the sidewalk. Well, I think that I was seeing his saying come to fruition.

The yard men had started to mow the lawn early because of the heat. Michael had watched me mow the lawn more than enough. He threw up his hands and hired a lawn service. I was right in assuming he would never be pleased with my mowing ability. I really think he was afraid I would have a heart attack because the heat that showed on my face and radiated from my entire body. Sweating was not very becoming. My face was bright red and my breath was nonexistent. He hired some lawn company with a name like "Lawns Are Us" or something like that, to mow the lawn at least through the summer. I was really glad because it was so hot that I didn't think I could have lasted a minute longer. Besides, I was born to sit under the veranda and drink a mint julep and watch someone else cut my grass. David would have agreed with that.

I used the extra time to get back into tennis. I really enjoyed tennis again. It was a great release. I got to play three or four times a week. I didn't do that when David was alive. I always felt that I needed to take better care of the house and have a hot meal on the table. We rarely went out to dinner because I preferred cooking for David. It took a long time to get back into shape. After David died I had lost lots of weight. Finding something to wear was difficult because everything hung on me like a sack. Finally, I was able to play without feeling like I couldn't breathe or my legs were going to buckle under me. There were times I had even felt I would have a heart attack. I was trying to work out a couple times a week without over doing it. Not over doing it was the easy part. Finally, I was hungry again. Eating had not been a priority.

One Thursday, that July, I had planned a really busy day. I was going to play tennis in the morning, have lunch with the girls and go to choir practice that evening. I had decided to join the choir again. I look back now and laugh when I thought that was a busy day.

I was a little nervous about going back to choir but at the same time I was excited. I hadn't felt that way in a long time. I did love to sing and I had missed it even though I didn't feel like I had anything to sing about, until then.

Reverend Doss seemed really pleased that I was coming back. His lovely wife was the choir director. I had figured if she found the strength to sing then I should. Their son had died about fifteen years before. They used their sadness to help others get through grief. I just can't imagine what a hole that must have put into their hearts. Even though they had lost a part of themselves they still seemed to have an inner glow. There are few people in the world that have that special aura about them. I saw the same thing in David and sometimes I would see it around Michael.

I found choir a wonderful release for me. If only for an hour I would feel like my old self.

Ann Doss possessed a special way of blending voices. I had never known anyone that had her amazing talent for blending music. She would position you next to someone that would compliment your voice rather than throw you off or overshadow your particular voice. There was one exception, Lilly Mooney. Bless her heart. She was ninety-three and still trying to sing. I wasn't sure that she could ever sing well. Her voice was crackly and she couldn't hear the key being played. I don't think even if she could have heard the key she would have been able to sing it. I stood by her once but Ann moved me because I kept getting tickled.

I am sure, when I turn ninety-three, someone will be saying the same thing about me. I hoped at ninety-three I would still be living and hopefully trying to sing, just not in the church choir.

Lilly still drove wherever she wanted to go. She drove a 1965 caddie. The wheel covers were missing and the gas flap was gone. She would brag that it only had sixty thousand miles on the odometer but it looked like it was on its last leg. I always gave her plenty of time to get home before leaving for my home because we traveled the same path. Once I did offer to pick her up but she would have none of that. I was a little afraid of driving close to her. There were so many dings in her car that the rust had become the permanent color. I was never, intentionally, getting in her path. She would always joke that her car lasted longer than any of her marriages. I think she was married four times and buried all four husbands. I wondered if one of them was the love of her life. I hoped that I could one day be as positive as Lilly. If I lived to be ninety, I wished that I would be as active as she. If my driving proves to be as poor as Lilly's, Michael better take my car keys away. Michael and I have had this discussion many times.

I think I was finally moving a little forward. Just a few months before I didn't see a future for me. I truly think that I felt as if a part of me died along with David. I guess in a sense that did happen. I still missed him enormously but the tears were less and I could see a small light at the end of the tunnel.

The nights were the hardest time for me. I tried to fill my days as much as possible so that by bedtime I would be exhausted and be able to sleep. One really silly thing I did was go out and buy one of those big body pillows. I would lay it next to me and somehow I would feel less lonely. I would put it behind me and close my eyes and pretend that David once again was sleeping next to me. I always thought that if a Psychiatrist got hold of that one he would have had a lot of reasons to have me committed. Was I crazy? Maybe. Was I lonely? Definitely.

It just seemed to be so unnatural not to be a part of a couple any more. I usually ate alone, drove to church alone and slept alone. The silence at times was almost deafening. I would find myself humming or doing laundry at strange times. The washing machine would drown out the quietness. I used to sing all the time when I worked around the house. I had begun to hum; maybe soon I will be in full voice.

I also found myself praying more. David prayed a lot. I used to tell him he prayed enough for the both of us. I think I was finally doing something that was helping me to heal and I knew that if David were watching he would be very pleased.

There were times I would start to pray and end up yelling at God. I'm still yelling but not as loudly. There were times that I would just start and cry for hours. Sometimes I would fall asleep crying. I finally got to the place that I would ask God to be patient with me. I know now just how patient He was, but He had to let me work through this my way, with His guidance. Which I now know was really His way of getting me through my grief and to rely on Him alone. I had never relied on God before; so, it was a long hard process. Being so new at this I faltered often.

I had come a long way but I knew that I had many miles to go. Somehow, someday, I had to find a way to heal.

I feel as if my father must have prayed in secret because he stayed in a loveless relationship for so long. He must have had something to keep him going because he never became angry or bitter. He still loved my mother even though she didn't love him. Maybe he felt like my mother was right in thinking he wasn't a good provider. He seemed to just go about life as if he were a robot, programmed to go through the motions without question. I'll never know because he never said anything. Daddy never complained.

When my father became sick, I truly think it was a relief to him. I know that he had grown weary of my mother's constant belittling him. I believe he was just tired of feeling like a failure. I never thought of him as a failure. To me he was a giant, a hero. I remember when my mother would go to bed I would crawl up into his lap and feel safe and loved. My father and David made me feel safe and comfortable. I kept that feeling deep inside of me. That was always what I would pull from when I needed strength. Maybe they relied on prayer. I know that when I pray I get that same feeling I did as a child in my father's lap. I hadn't thought of that feeling until David had died. I'm not sure that I welcomed this feeling because of the price I had to pay but I knew that somehow it was comforting even though I wished for someone's lap to crawl into and linger.

When my father died, I saw such peace on his face. There was a light in his eyes just before he breathed his last breath. That was a look that I had not ever seen on his wrinkled tired face before. Funny, as much as I loved my father, I really didn't know him because he never talked about himself. The one thing I do know was that he loved me with all of his heart.

I was so lucky when I met David. I got to leave my mother's reign. I did feel guilty leaving my brother and father. Though they were so happy for me and told me often. I felt like I had abandoned them but I was finally feeling safe. I never had felt so secure in my life.

When I was young I was always fearful of my mother's rage. She was so unpredictable. Even though, she didn't physically abuse any of us, she did mentally disfigure all of us. She was known to slap me but she never went further. I often wondered why she didn't go further than a face slap but somehow I felt lucky. Isn't that sad?

When I was growing up, I would tip toe around the house so that she would not notice me. If she noticed that I was around she would either yell at me or find some reason to slap me. She made Joe and I do all the work in the house. I knew that if I didn't do what she wanted us to do she would take it out on my dear father when he would come home in the evening. I loved him so much that I would do anything to keep her away from him. I never thought that he deserved her wrath, but he took it without any argument. He would listen to her rant and rave and then go on about his business. Poor Joe just tried to keep her happy by fixing her drinks and doing what she asked. He would even agree with her when she would talk about dad and me. I never got mad at him because I knew that he only did this so that she would love him. He tried so hard to make her love him but I don't think she knew how to love anything.

When Joe moved out after he had gotten married, mother was just horrible to him. Joe eloped so that mother wouldn't try to talk him out of it. She constantly interfered with his marriage and continued that hold she had on him. That marriage didn't last long. After my father died, he let her come to live with him and his second wife. That marriage crumbled quickly, as well. I really think even today his second wife, Sherry, still loves him. I know that Joe still loves her.

Mother convinced Joe to take care of her. In order to have her attention, he let her manipulate his entire life. I love my baby brother. He is a good guy like my father. He just doesn't know it.

"Thanks for the memories."

Chapter 8

Summer Takes Over

The first summer without David was one of the most hot and humid summers I had ever experienced. When I was growing up in southwest Virginia the temperatures were much more comfortable. I never went out in the evening without a light weight cotton sweater. Every young lady carried a white summer weight sweater when she left the house. When Joe and I were little I remember sleeping with the windows open and a fan blowing on us. We would wake up freezing in the middle of the night. You can't do that any more because things have built up so much that all of the buildings and asphalt hold in the summer heat.

Last summer, was no exception. The heat was stifling. I kept the house closed up because of the heat and humidity. I really missed the fresh air blowing through the windows. Though the dust was hard to keep up with, I never minded it.

Many of David's VMI friends had stopped by that summer. They treated me like family. I had also received many cards and letters; some from friends of David that I had never met. I guess when they call themselves brother rats they are truly brothers.

David's brother rats would sit and visit for hours. They would tell me stories about their crazy, sometimes dangerous, antics at school. Sometimes we would laugh and sometimes we would cry. David's friends really did miss him. I felt quite fortunate to be a part of this family. I was very grateful for their friendship and support.

Early in July, I was packing to go to the beach with Michael and Mary Lee. I was excited and happy that they had invited me to tag along. I wanted to spend as much time with my grandchildren as I could. I wanted to be the baby sitter and let them get out and spend time with each other. I had become aware of just how important time together was for them.

It had been a long time since I had been anywhere. I was really looking forward to a change of scenery. I had become somewhat of a recluse. It was all too easy to just exist. Thank goodness that I had tennis and choir to pass some of my time.

I was finding myself laughing again. Nine months had passed since David had died. Nine months of feeling like a heavy dark cloud was hanging over my head. I was still sad and at times angry. I knew that by getting away I would be able to put aside my sadness and feel less heart heavy. It would be a time to start focusing on the positives in my life.

I was tired of staying in bed, tired of crying and tired of feeling sorry for myself. I could see in the distance that candle of hope begin to flicker again. I had become very aware that life was so unpredictable and that I needed to capture and live each and every moment. And yes, I needed to thank God for everything that I had and not dwell on everything that I had lost. I never thought that I would see things this way and I never thought that I would get to a point that I would admit that there is a God.

I was never an atheist, I was too afraid to be. Deep down I knew He existed, I just didn't know where to find Him. I guess in my life it took a tragedy to start to look for God. It took David's death for me to realize that I needed God.

David and Michael were always so sure about God. I never knew how they had gotten to that point. It wasn't until I started praying that I realized that I, too, knew He was out there. There were times that I felt Him pat me on the back and tell me that He was there. It frightened me at first. I didn't know what was coming over me and I wasn't sure I wanted Him in my life. There were times that I still blamed God for what had happened. None the less, He would step in and tell me I was going to be alright. I think He was telling me to be patient and let Him remold me.

When I lost David, I was totally alone or so I thought. I had relied on David for everything. I had even let him be my direct line to God. Now that he was gone I had to find a way to survive. I had to reach out for God and I knew David was leading me to God and Heaven. I knew that I wanted to be with David again and I had to find the right path.

I would not say that religion had totally taken over my life because that would not be true. Hanna Fry was not a saint nor would I ever pretend to be. I knew that I needed something in my life. I knew that I had no earthly idea what but people much smarter than I kept telling me about God. I thought I should listen and open my mind to what they were telling me.

I had cried rivers of tears and I just didn't want to cry anymore. I look back now and think that was when God came to me and said for me to start living again. I think that was when I packed up my self pity and began walking in His light.

I finally finished packing and was in need of a good nights sleep. I knew that a ride to Myrtle Beach, South

Carolina was going to be loud and long with three children. I also had no idea of whether I would get any sleep for a week. So I tucked myself into bed and drifted off to what I thought was going to be a long, restful sleep.

Something jolted me awake. There was a sound like glass breaking coming from downstairs. I was trying to wake myself up enough so I could think. Without thinking I ran over to the bedroom door and pushed the dresser in front of it, just enough, so that the door wouldn't open. I have no idea how I moved the dresser because I am not a strong woman. I checked the house phone and found I couldn't dial out. My cell phone was by my bed. I quickly ran over and started to dial 911. I fumbled a few times but finally was able to dial. I should have had it programmed into my phone. My fingers would hardly work. When the dispatcher answered I told her someone had broken into my house. She wanted to know if I was safe and asked for my address. As I rambled she assured me that an officer was at the front of my house. She asked me if I thought anyone was still in my house but I wasn't sure of anything I was so frightened. I could see the lights of the police car in the front of my house. I ran over to look out the window and saw an officer chasing someone running down the sidewalk. Soon there were three cars in front of my house. I could see an officer coming up to the front door.

It wasn't as easy to push the chest of drawers away from the door as it was pushing it in front. I ran down the stairs to the front door. As I ran by the dining room I noticed the light was on and it was in shambles. I didn't stop but ran quickly to open the front door.

When I opened the front door there stood a policeman looking to be about twelve years old and resembling Opie on the Andy Griffith Show. He didn't look like Ron Howard when he was on Happy Days but a very young Ron Howard, a Ron Howard in puberty. Somehow that did not boost my confidence.

Later, an older officer came in. This time the officer looked at least thirty. That helped a little. They began to look through the house. The dining room seemed to be his target. The intruder had broken the glass in the back door and reached down and unlocked the deadbolt. In a flash he was in my house. He must have cut himself because there was blood everywhere.

Opie had gone outside to look around. When he came back inside, he was holding the cut phone line. At that time there were no underground utilities in my neighborhood. He had easy access to the phone line and to my house. My old house was at least seventy-five years old. The neighborhood was tree lined and older. I doubt if ever there could be underground lines put in because of all the tree roots.

It seemed like and eternity since I had called Michael and Joe to come over but finally they were there. I felt so much safer when they arrived. They took over talking with the officers. Opie told them what had happened. While they were talking, Opie's radio called to tell him that they had caught the man a few blocks down the street. The resident dog had pointed him out. It seemed he was hiding in a trash can and holding a bag of my silver and a small bag of gold coins that I had completely forgotten about. David had not been much of a collector but he loved the intricacy of these coins. He had collected around twenty of these little gems. I had no idea of their worth.

I laughed at the whole situation under my breath, of course. I think that was purely a nervous reaction. I didn't want to think about how frightened I was just a short time before.

Here I was a widowed woman, living alone and I had never even thought of being afraid but I was stunned by my fear.

In an instant, I went from a lonely widowed woman to a frightened mess. I thought of how afraid I was and realized that the fear was paralyzing. I still to this day don't know why I reacted the way I did but I did know it wasn't me reacting. My quick thinking didn't come from me but from somewhere or someone else.

Michael insisted that I go home with him. I was already packed so I quickly jumped at the chance. Joe had offered to stay at the house with his boxer, Dempsey, and take care of everything. He promised to clean and fix all the mayhem. Again, the men in my life came to my rescue.

This would be an opportunity for Joe to get away from mother. He needed sometime to himself and this was his brief moment of escape. I wasn't so sure that Dempsey was a good idea but I knew Joe did not go anywhere without him. Mother wouldn't have taken care of him anyway. She never liked animals although she did let us have a kitten for a while but Fluffy ran away. She was really smart to get out of our mess.

Before I left I wrote a brief statement for the police and thanked them for their help. I was out of there as quickly as I could move.

I was then on my way to be grandmother extraordinaire, a role that I had begun to put my heart and soul into.

"The only thing we have to fear is fear itself."
-Franklin Delano Roosevelt

Chapter 9

An Ocean of Hope

The drive to the beach took nine hours. It should have taken five and a half or six hours, but with eight potty breaks, it took forever. When one of the children would have to stop, the others didn't. I really think Michael was the worst. Looking back on it, I think it was the ten cups of coffee he drank. Every time we would stop he would get another cup. He probably needed it to stay awake because of being up so late the night before.

Michael had gotten a new van for the trip. There were movies to watch and video games to play. The girls traveled much better than Lyle. He was as rambunctious as he could be. We had to give him a seat by himself so that no one would touch him. So he sat there like a king on a throne, wiggling and griping all the way. I think the excitement of going to the beach had gotten the best of him. Maybe it was just because boys can't sit still for very long. No one could be mad at him because he had two little dimples that would melt the hardest heart.

I was having trouble getting the break-in off my mind. I felt so violated. How dare a stranger come into my house and go through my things. I can say now that the worst part was how much fear he had instilled in me. I'm glad that I'll never know what would have happened if I had not heard him. I wondered what he would have done if he had made his way up the stairs. Thank goodness he didn't and I will never know.

As we drove south I stared out of the window. I didn't notice much of anything. Everything I saw seemed like a big blur. As we drove I continued to stare until my eyes were stinging. I don't think I blinked for hours.

The police department called Michael's cell phone early that morning to tell him that the guy was someone they had been looking for many months. There had been a number of break-ins in town and all of them were happening to widows. They speculated he had gotten names from the newspaper and cased the houses for a while picking just the right time. The strange thing was that he picked times that the women were home. He must have gotten a charge scaring them to death. Fortunately, he hadn't hurt anyone. No, he hadn't hurt anyone physically but mentally he had done incredible damage.

I couldn't help but think of the women that didn't have cell phones. They must have just been as horrified as he went through their things and wondering what he would do next. I felt so helpless. I was finally getting strong again and then that happened. I tried to fight back the tears so that the children didn't see them. This was just one more reminder that I was a widow. Widow, a word I thought I would never have to use, a word that really had never been a part of my vocabulary.

Finally, we arrived and in an instant calmness came over me. The beach house was so beautiful. The décor was all blue and white, and the floors where a sandy colored carpet. It truly looked like something out of a magazine. I fell in love with it immediately. I think my favorite place was the back porch, with its heavy wooden rockers and a Pawley's Island hammock strung from the rafters. Wouldn't David have loved that hammock? The porch overlooked the ocean. The dunes were full of sea grass that waved as the wind blew through them. The grasses were so graceful. If you watched them for very long I think they could hypnotize you. I felt like a child seeing the ocean for the first time because my excitement was hard to contain. The air smelled so fresh and new.

The boardwalk almost went from the house to the ocean. I had never stayed in Litchfield before. South Carolina has so many beautiful beaches. David and I had always stayed where the most golf courses were. Michael didn't even bring his clubs. He wanted this to be a total family vacation. Besides he and Mary Lee played golf at home together most every Sunday afternoon. Most of the time they only played nine holes but time alone was what it was all about.

I never cared if David wanted to play golf because it gave me lots of time to sit on the beach and read a good summer novel about trashy women and their nightly escapades.

I had noticed that I was always hungrier at the beach. Just the thought of fried seafood would make my mouth water. I really did need to eat because over the past few months I had lost a lot of weight. I think I must have looked frail because people would see me and ask if I had been sick. Not to worry, I was sure that after this week I would be back to my former weight and then some.

I really didn't care what I looked like anyway. I had given up wearing bikinis a long time ago. There was nothing sexy about a fifty something year old woman. I hadn't thought about what I looked like for a long time. When I looked in the mirror I didn't see me. I saw a very sad woman with dark circles under her eyes. I really didn't pay attention to my looks. Now, when I think about it, I really had let myself go.

Most of the nights, while we were on vacation, I cooked in because it was hard to take the children out and enjoy the meal. Mary Lee and Michael wanted to help but I found pleasure in going to the market and planning a great meal for us. The cooking was very therapeutic. I wanted to help out as much as I could because I was so grateful that they had invited me to go with them. Besides, I wanted Michael and Mary Lee to have a vacation and I wanted, once again, to feel needed.

I always thought how lucky I was that Michael had chosen Mary Lee for a wife. They met while Michael was in college. Michael had dated one girl all through high school. She was a year younger than he. When he graduated he broke up with her. He wanted the full experience of college without being tied down. He met Mary Lee his junior year and that was it. He fell head over heels and so did she. They waited to get married after they both graduated. I think David and I were surprised when we first met her. So was so different from anyone Michael had ever been interested in.

She was not at all pretentious. She was very down to earth. She would have every right to be a little uppity, because she has brains, beauty and talent. I guess I should be a little jealous of her, but Michael says he married someone just like his mother. I think he married the perfect life partner. She and I have always had a good relationship. I am very proud of both of them and consider her my child. She takes wonderful care of my son. What more could a mother want?

One of the nights at the beach, we went to the pavilion to ride rides and eat junk. The children rode everything and ate cotton candy and drank frozen lemonade until they almost popped. They fussed when it was time to go but when we left the parking lot they were all three fast asleep. When we got back to the house we carried them in and tucked them in their cozy little beds. I suggested that Michael and Mary Lee go for a walk on the beach. I remembered those long midnight walks that David and I took. We would walk for hours not aware of the time and the fact that we would have to walk back. That was another place and another time.

I would watch the ocean for hours each morning before everyone would awaken. In and out, back and forth, so constant, the ocean never stops. You can always depend on it. Some people plan their day around it and some plan their livelihood around it. I planned my emotional healing around it.

One early morning, just before dawn, I went for a long walk. While walking, my emotions took over and I started to cry. Old memories had flooded my mind. I began to cry uncontrollably. As I cried I walked further into the ocean. I was totally unaware of how far I had wandered into the water when a large wave came crashing down on me, knocking me to the ground. I was so surprised that I couldn't react. I kept trying to get up as another wave would come and knock me down again. The harder I tried the worse it got. Then, I started to laugh at how awkward I must have looked. I think God was telling me to stop looking behind and look ahead. I think in his way he was saying when a wave knocks you down get up, laugh, live and love. There will be many waves in your life and if you let them keep you down you will drown. I looked to Heaven and said, "Alright, I get it you've made your point."

David, I am sure, was in Heaven just rolling. I know that he would have found my flounder impression really funny.

God washed me clean that day. My life changed. My outlook changed. Yes, most important my heart changed. I knew that I had so many things of which I needed to let go. I knew I had to go home to Virginia and start living again not as Mrs. David Fry but as Hanna Devon Fry. I knew that I needed more in my life; I just didn't know exactly what. I did know that with God's help I would find it. Maybe not the next day or even in a year but I would find it.

Before we left the beach I took a ride with a realtor. David had always wanted to buy a place in Pinehurst. He had planned on retiring at sixty. He didn't ever get to relax and enjoy the fruits of his labor. He had never said that he wanted a place at the beach but I thought it would be alright with him if I bought a small beach retreat. I even thought that he would applaud my spunk.

We looked for hours at million dollar properties but I couldn't see spending everything on a house or a small piece of land.

As we were riding around in Pawley's Island, I spotted a small, run down cottage that was for sale. I told the realtor I wanted to see it but she insisted that it was just a mess and should be torn down. She thought of it as an eyesore but I saw it as a jewel. It looked like me. I was shabby, in disrepair and I needed a lot of work. What could have been more perfect for me? This was truly a match made in heaven. Finally, I saw a hobby for me, fixing up both of us. I laughed and thought that it may not be a hobby but a full time job. So I bought the little cottage.

I didn't tell Michael where I had been. I told him that I had been site seeing. That wasn't a lie. I had truly seen sites that I had never seen before. I knew that Michael would try to talk me out of my little Shabby Place. I had already given it a name. That was when I knew I was attached.

All I could think of was the next summer coming down for three months to work on my house. This was a new focus for me other than my loss. I had found a new beginning, not an ending. I felt as if I had bought a little piece of paradise. We even looked alike. We were meant to be together. Had it been fate or divine intervention? I don't know but I knew it was right.

"A cleansing wave for a broken heart."

Chapter 10

Home Sweet Home

After stopping at every outlet along the way and every fruit stand with homemade peach ice cream, we, finally, made it home. I could see our waistlines grow.

The ridges of the mountains truly were blue and seemed to welcome us home with opened arms. There is something comforting about their majesty.

Joe was there waiting for me and his trusty dog, Dempsey, greeted me with a slobbery lick.

Joe had repaired my back door and had an alarm system installed. There were stickers on the window and signs in the yard. It surely was a beacon telling all burglars not to try this house. I told him all that wasn't necessary but down deep I was relieved. I needed to renew my since of security.

I could tell Joe and Michael wanted to tell me something. They just kept looking at each other and then back at me. Finally, I couldn't stand it any longer so I asked why they were acting so mysterious.

They must have been talking all week while we were at the beach and devising their plans. Their story was well thought out and planned. Neither one of them could keep silent any longer.

Michael started with that caring son voice he had used in many other occasions when he was trying to get me to do something that he knew very well I wouldn't want to do. They had decided what was good for me without asking me what I thought but I listened intently to their scheme.

In a nut shell, they wanted Joe and Dempsey to move into the apartment over the garage. Joe chimed in with his plan of taking care of the yard and doing all of the maintenance on the house. He was also convinced that his slobbery ball of fur would be a good watch dog. They continued, on and on, while I listened.

Finally, I began to smile, which I think annoyed them. Then I said something which stopped them in their tracks.

I asked a question that they seemed to have forgotten about. I asked them what they were going to do with mother. I realized that they didn't want me to go there. Their faces grew white and their mouths dropped. I certainly wasn't going to offer for her to come live here with me and they knew that.

I figured they either hadn't told her or she wasn't happy with all of this. I didn't have to worry because I was pretty sure that she wouldn't want to live with me.

Joe spoke up and said that it was time he took control of his own life. He was great at talking about things but I knew that mother would go ballistic and Joe would cave.

I was also very sure that mother would blame me again for sabotaging their relationship. Somehow it would be my fault that David died and all of this was taking place. Mother had always been miserable and she wanted company. Unfortunately my little brother, Joe, drew the shortest straw.

Nothing more was said about Joe moving in and life went on as usual. There were times I was still uneasy at night but I had come to the realization that too would go away.

August arrived so quickly. It seemed summer had just begun but I knew it was soon to be over. I wanted to pack in as many summertime things as I could. I would go by often and pick up the grandchildren. We had picnics on the Blue Ridge Parkway; we played miniature golf and swam. Mary Lee was so happy because it gave her some alone time. Not that she would have ever complained about not having time to herself.

Little did I know she was interviewing for a part time job as a school nurse. When she and Michael were first married she had worked as a nurse for a couple of years, but as soon as Lyle was born she became a full time mother. Now that all three children would be in school she decided to go back to work. Sarah was to start kindergarten that fall so it was a perfect opportunity.

One afternoon after having the children, Joe stopped by. He looked as if he had seen a ghost. I couldn't imagine what could have been wrong. He came in and sat at the kitchen table while I fixed a pot of coffee. Joe drank coffee during the day and Bourbon at night.

He began to tell me that while I was at the beach mother had been in a lot of pain but refused to go to the doctor. She always hated doctors because they would lecture her about her drinking and smoking. She never trusted doctors or anyone else for that matter.

He told me that a few days before he had found her on the floor of the bathroom doubled over in pain. He took her immediately to the emergency room. Mother not wanting to spend money refused any tests the doctors said needed to be done but Joe had insisted and she was in too much pain to argue.

I was almost angry that Joe had not called me but he said that mother didn't want me to know anything. I believed that because she had always shut me out of her life.

Joe kept apologizing for mother but I knew it was the same old story. Why should I have thought that this time should be different?

Joe told me they had kept mother in the hospital for a couple of days to run a battery of test. The doctor had called Joe that morning to tell him to come in because he wanted to talk with him. Joe said it sounded serious and he needed me to go with him. I was a little hesitant because mother would not want me there but Joe said he couldn't do it alone. He said that he needed me. I knew we needed each other just as we did when we were children.

I never thought that I would have had any emotion when it came to my mother. There were times growing up that I would pretend that she died. I don't think that I really wanted her to die, I just wanted her to be normal but that would be wishing for the impossible.

I did feel emotion. I can't describe what I felt. I just know that I was feeling as if I couldn't breathe. I guess I really thought that she would never be sick and I had never ever thought that she would someday die. I just thought that she would always be there to torment me.

That afternoon, Dr. Justice told us that mother had six months to live. He told Joe and me that she was in the final stage of liver cancer. He felt that anyone in her condition should be kept at home with family rather than in a nursing facility because her time was limited and she needed to be with loved ones. He kept looking at me while he talked. He told me if she wanted a drink of liquor that I should give it to her. The damage was done and it probably would help with her pain. I asked him why he was telling me this because mother lived with Joe. The doctor turned to Joe and asked him if he had discussed any of this with me.

Joe began by telling me that he and the doctor had already spoken on the phone. He told me that she would need constant care and he couldn't give it to her because he would be at work during the day. He also said he would never be able to change her diapers when she got to that point. I hadn't thought of any of that. I had just been bombarded with the fact that my mother was dying and she needed to die in my home. I think I felt as if someone had just punched me in the chest. I didn't know what to say or how to react. What kind of person would I be if I said no?

The doctor told me that Hospice could be of some service. They would help especially at the end with her medications.

Joe very quietly told me this was my opportunity to heal my wounds. He said that it was time mother and I had a relationship. I sat there in a daze. I wondered how he knew what was best for me. Joe didn't know what was best for him and certainly not me.

I remembered when I was a child and would see movies with mothers and daughters relying on each other. I would pretend that the woman in the movie was my mother. I would dream about a loving mother only to awaken to my reality.

I remembered being so jealous of the girl across the street, Brenda Sue and her mother. They were always hugging. They loved each other. I so wanted that relationship with my mother.

Finally, I spoke up and told the doctor to make the arrangements for mother to come home with me. I couldn't believe that I was saying those words but I did and still don't know why.

I knew that my mother would be upset and not want me to take care of her. I knew it would be an uphill climb and I didn't have much time to climb that hill.

After a week in the hospital, mother came home with me. She wasn't very happy about the whole situation and let me know every minute how she felt. There was no miracle change. I had truly hoped for a movie ending but it looked like my mother wasn't going to budge.

Four weeks passed and mother became increasingly weaker. I had been fixing her meals but she had just stopped eating. She wasn't asking for a drink anymore. I think that she had given up on life. Her voice had become very quiet and so had her personality. As she wasted away so did her nastiness. When she needed something she would even say please.

Joe was coming by less and less. He just couldn't watch her waste away. I think that he was afraid to watch her go. He would call everyday but that was about it. I didn't need his help which surprised me. Mother had become not a burden but a part of my routine.

Joe would call and tell me he loved me and then he would have to go. I really know now that Joe was finding a new independence. For fifty years, my mother had been his life. No one could blame him because he had been so dedicated to her for most of his life.

As mother grew sicker, I would read to her. I read books and magazine articles but one morning I picked up the Bible and read to her. She didn't resist so I continued to read it to her everyday. I knew that I needed to read it for myself. She seemed to listen and I think she was taking it all in. There were times I even saw her cry. She didn't want me to see so I never called attention to it. I had never seen my mother cry before. She looked so frail and helpless. As I watched her waste away and loose her strength, I grew stronger.

It had been five weeks and her pain was increasing. I called Joe to tell him that hospice had said it was time for her to go on morphine. I had dreaded that day because I knew she would just sleep until she died and, for once, I had a mother. It had taken years for me to be able to hold my mother's hand. I had longed for a mother and I finally felt that mother-daughter bond. I didn't want to give that up.

The day Hospice came to give her morphine, Joe and I gathered to say our goodbyes. We really thought that she would linger for a while longer but not be able to hear us or know that we were there. We wanted her to hear us one more time. As we held her hand, she asked me to pray for her. I think that was the first time I had ever prayed for someone and I know it was the first time I had prayed aloud. Joe even prayed as we said the Lord's Prayer. Funny, I didn't know he knew it.

The nurse gave her the shot and as it began to flow through her veins she asked me to come closer so I did. She whispered to me. She slipped into a deep sleep. I truly saw God soften her heart and carry her spirit to heaven. Her body lasted for a few more days but God had relieved her of her pain and agony on this earth.

We buried her next to my dad on a cold September morning. Not many people came because she didn't have any friends. The people that did come were friends of Michael's and mine. Joe's second wife came to support him though I'm sure that it was hard for her to come. They came out of respect for us and I was happy to see my friends. Reverend Doss spoke many beautiful, comforting words. He hadn't known my mother long but he found words especially about my mother. He spoke about her in the last few months and didn't mention her past because it was just that, the past.

The loss wasn't like my loss of David. I had found closure. I was able to make peace with my mother. I felt like a different person. I felt stronger. I felt as if that black cloud was lifted off me.

I didn't wear black to mother's funeral. I felt like it was a celebration. Joe and I both were relieved… somewhat. Not because she was gone but because we felt that she was finally happy. I hoped that God accepted her because I think that in the end she accepted Him.

My mother had a hold on our emotions for a long time. I would see mother's smile at their children when I was growing up and I really can't remember my mother ever smiling at me until right before she died. I really don't think I ever smiled at her when I was growing up either.

I spent my childhood afraid of making my mother angry. When she was angry she would drink more and yell at all of us. My father and I were the ones that would set her off. Joe always sat back and watched as she would lash out. Even as a child he was able to calm her down. He could talk her into going to her room. I'm sure she would tell him all kinds of awful things about my father and me. Sometimes to just get her calm he would agree. Dad and I both knew that he didn't believe those things and that Joe loved us dearly.

Joe and I had a tight bond. We have endured more than most brothers and sisters. He is in my heart and I in his.

I thought that I would resent taking care of my mother because she never took care of me but that wasn't the case. I found something in me that I didn't know existed. I found that with God's help I could forgive my mother and even love her.

"To forgive is to forget."

Chapter 11

Turning Over a New Leaf

The August heat had turned into an ideal September warmth. The colors of fall hadn't begun to turn on the mountains. I have always had such excitement for fall. That time of the year makes me feel warm and cozy. It's a feeling of wrapping up in a fluffy old quilt on a cool fall night. Even as a child I loved the fall. I was always excited to start school. I loved school because it was the one place where I felt I belonged or maybe it was a safe escape. It was a place where I could pretend that everything in my life was normal. I was waiting excitedly for the trees to put forth their magnificent colors before retiring for their winter's nap.

One afternoon, Michael came over for coffee. While we were visiting, he reminded me of one of David's favorite sayings. When he would have an occasional cigar while sitting on the deck he would throw out his arms and shout," there is a God. Look at his art work." We would laugh and talk about when Michael was little. When the leaves would change color in the fall, he would call them "Fruity Pebbles". That had always made a great impression on us because every fall we said the same old thing.

I was planning a big celebration for next month. It was going to be a year since David had passed away. I had been so lost and sad for so many months that all I could think of was my loss. I finally had come out of the dark and wanted the world to know just how much I appreciated the time that I had spent with David. I felt that I was a better person for being able to have him pass through my life. I had been told that God places people and events in our lives for a purpose. If I had to guess, David's purpose in my life was to set me on the right path, both spiritually and emotionally. I am such a different person now than I was eleven months ago and much different than when I was a young girl. If I had any regrets, one would be the fact that David did not see the changes I had made in my life. I have gained an inner strength that I never thought I had. If what everyone says is true, I guess he can see from heaven. We had a grand life together and it was time for us to celebrate his life on earth.

It had taken me a month but I finally had told Michael about the beach house. He already knew. Mr. Price at the bank slipped and told him. I really don't think he slipped, I think he was so worried I had lost my mind and he wanted Michael to check me in somewhere. Michael never made any type of a comment. He shook his head and smiled. I think I continually surprised him.

The children had started school already and Mary Lee had begun working part time as a nurse at their school. I think the school system is so lucky to have her. I am sure she will be there for a long time because I know Mary Lee loves her career and this is an ideal job for her. I have always marveled at her patience and love for children.

I am volunteering one morning a week at their school. The elementary school has a grandparent reading program; so, Mary Lee signed me up. Most of the children come from single parent homes. A large number of the parents work full time; so, when it comes to homework and reading they just don't have much energy left. This was a great job for me because I love to read. Besides, I got a lot out of it. Their faces just make me feel like I'm doing something that matters.

I was finding myself more involved in the community. All of this started out as a way to occupy my time and it has turned into a very important part of my life. Before, David took up a lot of my time and thoughts. He needed me more than I ever realized. I always thought that I was the one in need but he also needed me. Our life was symbiotic. I had to find a way to rely on myself and this past year I have learned just that. I didn't have a choice.

Your life can change in an instant. I think God challenges us to adjust to those changes. Some of us adjust, even grow; and some choose to pine away in their own misery. I came very close to pining away. I remember staying in bed most mornings without a desire to get up. There were times that I would cry my eyes out and then cry some more. I don't really remember when I stopped feeling sorry for myself. It just happened.

I remember a woman at church saying to me that in time I would feel better. I hated her at the time. I didn't want to feel better. I know that she was right. Time did heal the pain. Oh, don't get me wrong, I will always love David and I will miss him forever but now I can look back and smile at our time together. My tears are few, my memories are sweet and, yes, life does go on.

As a family, we decided to throw a party as a celebration of David's life. I had tended to every detail of the party. I had ordered all the food and hired the servers. No one turned down the invitation, everyone was coming. So many people wanted to celebrate David's life and didn't want to miss a good party. He was a wonderful person and will be missed by many. Heaven is a much brighter place with him there.

I looked around at my big house and sometimes felt overwhelmed. I thought about my little Shabby House and knew it was calling me to come and fix it up. My heart skipped a beat when I thought about it. I daydreamed about a new beginning and a new challenge.

I had to get myself back on task and finish the details of the party. I did find staying on task more difficult. So many things reminded me of what used to be.

I needed to shop for a new dress. I hadn't bought anything to wear in so long and I was a little excited to go shopping. Believe me; I was not going to wear black. I thought that I would look for an orange dress. That is a great fall color. Then I came to my senses. What was I thinking? I probably would look like a pumpkin; so, I had to just look around for "that" perfect dress.

The party had come and gone; it was everything that I wanted it to be. Michael and Joe toasted and roasted David. They brought up happy memories and didn't dwell on the sadness. Some of his college friends came and told funny stories about their times together. I hadn't heard some of the tales but I did learn that David wasn't so perfect after all. Funny thing, just when you think you know someone. Everyone will miss him a great deal, but we all are better people just for knowing him.

Having this party was the best thing I could have done for both Michael and myself. There were times that I had forgotten that Michael had lost his father. I had been wrapped up in my own grief. Michael shared his feelings with me for the first time in a year. I guess he felt that he had to be strong for me and I didn't even notice his hurt. The healing process has taken a long time for the both of us; but, none the less, we are heading in the right direction.

I, finally, went to the cemetery. It had been since mother's funeral. I took the flowers from the party and placed them on David's and my parent's graves. I told them that I loved them and I said my final goodbyes. I had been afraid to say goodbye. I don't know why, maybe I thought it made me feel defeated. What was amazing was that it made me feel relieved. Why I felt relief, I don't know. Maybe I finally gave myself permission to move on.

The year passed a lot faster than I thought it would. After fifty, the years pass so quickly. David has been gone for a full year. Today is the anniversary of his death. A year ago I thought I would be sad forever. Sad isn't the word to describe what I feel now. I do miss him so much. He was always an inspiration to me and to many others that his life touched. He has left a grand legacy.

The scholarship that he endowed for VMI was given to a tremendous young man. I was so impressed with his demeanor and just how mature a 19 year old man conducted himself. Of course, I have always been impressed with most everyone who attended VMI. They enter as boys and girls and graduate as fine adults.

This year has been quite a learning year for my whole family. Michael has blossomed into a wonderful businessman, much like his father. His father's traits are so evident. I watch him sometimes and can't tell the difference from afar. What strong genes David had passed on to our son. I am so proud of my son. He is a wonderful son, husband and father. There's nothing more a mother could ask of her son.

Joe, what can I say about Joe? He moved in with me to help. Yes, he helped me around the house but he truly helped me in so many other ways. Without his insistence I would not have discovered my mother's heart and in doing that, I healed old wounds. Finally, after all these years I realized that we can't change who our parents are but we can accept them for who they are. I spent years trying to convince myself that all my problems stemmed from my mother. When, in actuality, they stemmed from me feeling sorry for myself. I never knew that I could go to God and begin again and leave the past behind. My brother is a good man and he now knows it. He is my baby brother and I love him with all my heart. His forgiving nature always made his goodness shine.

I realized that I have been trying to make my mother something she was not. My mother was my mother. She had flaws and so do I. I see my mother in me at times. I always wanted to be like my father but Joe is more like my dad. I blamed my mother for everything that went wrong in my life. After watching her become so helpless and need me more and more, I just realized that I had to let go of the past and learn to forgive her. Her illness challenged me to become a better person. I learned my mother was my mother, flaws and all. When mother died I was almost relieved. Not because she was gone but because I knew she too had found something in me that she never had taken time to notice. She found out that she loved me and told me so just before she died. She pulled me close and whispered she loved me.

This has been a year of tears, fears, and cheers. I have come a long way and have a long way to go. I have learned that the best traveling companion is God. He will carry you through anything. I am just sorry it took me so many years to find him. I thank him everyday for the opportunity to have met David. His spirit lives on in me and through Michael. He touched my life with his goodness and I hope that when my last day comes that someone will say that about me.

"There is no time like the present."

Chapter 12

Year Two

It's been a while since I have written in my journal. I have been so busy this year. The changes in my life have been enormous.

When November came Michael and I were still recovering from the big party we threw celebrating David's life. So many people said it was the best party they had ever attended. We danced until the wee hours of the morning. People stayed way past midnight. I hadn't stayed up that long in months but I loved every minute of it. David would have surely approved of his tribute. I am sure if he was watching, he was a little embarrassed by it all. He never wanted anyone to make a fuss over him.

November was such a beautiful month. The temperature was between fifty and sixty degrees. Thanksgiving Day we were able to sit out on the patio. That was great because the children could run and jump all they wanted. Since I had not cooked anything the year before, I decided to cook the whole meal. I know that Mary Lee was very happy because with working, her time was short.

Everyone told me their favorite thing and I accommodated each one. Of course, we had a twenty pound turkey with all the trimmings. Lyle wanted creamed corn and Sissy wanted green beans. Sarah wanted chocolate pie and homemade rolls. Michael and Mary Lee wanted me to make ambrosia and Joe wanted mashed potatoes. Joe's second wife, Sherry, came and she wanted me to make my cheesecake. It was a real feast and we ate way too much. After lunch, we went inside and sat around like slugs while the children ran around and burned off calories. We all laughed and said that was what we needed to be doing but not a one of us moved from our chairs.

Joe and Sherry had been dating again. I hadn't seen him so happy in a long time. He was drinking less and smiling more. Sherry is really good for him even though mother didn't think so. Mother really didn't want to share him with anyone. In her eyes, he belonged to her and no one could have him but her.

Michael and Mary Lee made a truly unexpected announcement that day. Michael was acting like a little kid that was about to burst with a secret. He and Mary Lee announced that they were expecting their fourth child. I was shocked because Mary Lee had just gone back to work. Mary Lee said she was just as surprised as we were but really excited. They were expecting another boy and wanted to name him David. Needless to say, I was thrilled. A new baby was just what this family needed.

It was a very special Thanksgiving and we had a lot to be thankful for. I had finally come to a place in my life that I could focus on what I have and not what I lost.

Michael was running David's business with great zeal. He seemed to move into David's space and not miss a beat. The employees were extremely helpful, but Michael had been with David since graduating from college, so he knew the drill. I would have never told him but I think Michael is a bit more creative than David.

With another child on the way, Michael and Mary Lee had a lot to think about. Their house was only a three bedroom, with one and a half bathrooms. It was a great starter home but with four children, they would be very over crowded. They had begun the search for a new house.

Every time they had an appointment to look at a house, I would keep the children. They loved to come to grandma's house. Lyle loved all of the secret hiding places. Some of my closets had small doors cut into them to get to the eve storage. To a little boy it was like a cave. I remembered Michael loved the little escape hatches, as he called them. One day while I was keeping the children, Lyle suggested that they move in with me. Well, that got me to thinking. Out of the mouth's of babes. Now that is an understatement. What a perfect idea.

The more I thought about Lyle's idea the more it made sense. My house had four bedrooms and two bathrooms upstairs and a small bedroom and bathroom downstairs. It was a great house for them and really too big for one old lady. Besides, my little Shabby Place was calling me. Winter was just around the corner so I needed to make up my mind soon. How would I approach Michael with my idea? He would have to go for it because it's perfect for the both of us.

As excited as I was, I found that I was also a little reluctant to change. Changes were all about me and I was pretty overwhelmed. I told Michael and Mary Lee about the idea and how Lyle came up with it. I thought if I threw in that it was Lyle's idea, they might be more acceptant toward it.

They thought about it for about a day and then told me it was what they were hoping. When I told them I would be going to South Carolina for the winter, they almost decided not to buy my house because they thought they were uprooting me. I think they thought I would be staying in town and buying a condo. I reminded them that I don't do anything conventional anymore. It's just to keep them on their toes.

Joe and Sherry were together again and living in her house so the garage apartment was empty. I told Michael that would be my home away from home from now on. I decided what to move into the apartment and what to put in storage for my new South Carolina home. Christmas was coming soon and I wasn't going to move until sometime in January. We began the moving process for Michael and his family before Christmas. This old house was getting a new lease on life. In a lot of ways, I was getting a new lease on life also. I felt like Hanna Devon Fry was growing up and becoming somewhat independent.

Even though I was excited, I was really nervous about leaving my safe, familiar surroundings of some fifty years. I had never done anything on my own before buying that little house. I was starting to doubt my sanity. I had no idea where to start or what to do, but I was about to find out. I was going to rebuild an old house, not knowing that I was going to rebuild me.

As I began to pack my treasures, I noticed what a pack rat I had become. I had saved so many things Michael had drawn as a child. I hadn't seen these things for years but it seemed like only yesterday that I had opened mother's day cards written by a seven year old. I could remember every freckle on his rosy cheeks. I could even remember the dirty little fingers handing me his card that he had poured his heart into. I could not ever part from these little treasures. I repacked the little box of cards and pictures and wrote on the top what they were. Then I neatly taped the box shut and tucked it back into the closet. I knew that at sometime Lyle would find the box and would pour over each piece of paper and love the fact that his father had once been a little boy.

As the years pass, we tend to forget little details of the days, but by keeping all my little treasurers, my memory is triggered and the details flow over me once again.

I had never worked so hard in all my life trying to decide what to take to the apartment, what to move to South Carolina and what to leave for Michael and Mary Lee.

Michael and Mary Lee didn't have a lot of furniture and with five bedrooms they would need more. I decided to leave the guestroom furniture in the downstairs bedroom for them. It had been in David's family for generations and I really thought Michael would naturally be the one to inherit it. This was the bed in which David was born. I think his father was born in this bed as well. It was massive and I really hated to move it anyway. Michael was so pleased that he was now the bedroom furniture caretaker.

As the weather turned colder, we had completed the move in portion of our change, but as far as being settled, that was not close to being completed. To tell you the truth, I don't think that will ever be the case. I was starting to feel a little like a gypsy. I was more overwhelmed than I thought I would be. I guess I thought that everything would just fall into place, but living out of boxes was not easy and I was starting to get tired of it. I was beginning to feel the need to get on my way south and after Christmas, I was going to spread my wings.

As December made its way in, it brought a definite change in the weather. There was crispness in the air. Of course, the day after Thanksgiving the children were ready for Christmas. The stores around town had been decorated in the holiday spirit since the day after Halloween. The Salvation Army bells had been ringing all year, I think.

At least it seemed that way. Though the bells annoyed me a little, it wouldn't be Christmas without their ringing. I always managed to find some change to drop in the little red pots.

I was starting to get excited about my new adventure. Things seemed so new to me now. The apartment was fine and it looked like home. The main house was so fresh looking but still felt like I had a place there. The kids things made it look as if it had a new purpose. I loved looking at the toys and Lego's all over the house. If houses have feelings I know that this old house was bursting with happiness. It was filled with the voices of little angels and about to have another little angel descend upon it. Michael and Mary Lee were starting all of their traditions where I had started my family traditions and that made me so very happy. I knew that David was with us because I could see his influence in so many things that Michael did. Once again, life was good.

"Our house is a very, very, very fine house."
-Crosby, Stills, Nash and Young

Chapter 13
Family Christmas Album

Christmas morning came early in the Fry house. The girls were up by six a.m. and Lyle was not far behind. Before going to bed, Michael told them not to go downstairs because he wanted to get the camera ready and Mary Lee needed to put the coffee on. Like good little children they sat at the top of the stairs about to burst. I had stayed in the guestroom so not to miss a second of the excitement. Michael kept flitting around trying to build the excitement until I told him to hurry up because I was about to explode. With one flash of the camera the children bolted for the living room. Their eyes were as big as saucers.

Santa had left a dome tent for camping and, yes, it was set up. There were many colorful trucks and a Gameboy for Lyle. The girls had gotten the latest craze in dolls and even play makeup. Sissy went for the wrapped boxes. She had looked at them under the tree long enough and she was ready to open presents. Sarah wasn't far behind her but Lyle had already started to play his Gameboy and didn't want to stop. I could see that this could present a problem because

Michael was not going to let him play it all day long. Finally, he put it down so the festivities could begin.

Mary Lee appeared from the kitchen with a lighted birthday cake. Everyone stopped what they were doing and wondered what this was all about. When she put the cake on the table she had written on the top "Happy Birthday Jesus." I thought she was such a good mother and wished I had thought of it. We sang "Happy Birthday" and started a new tradition in the new Fry home. I think for the first time ever we ate cake for breakfast. I thought to myself that this old house was in for wonderful times.

Naturally, we had everyone in the family over to eat Christmas dinner. We ate too much and we all moaned the rest of the day. I looked out of the window about five o'clock and snow was beginning to fall. I don't think that Christmas could have been more perfect. Then, I realized that my David wasn't there. I had tried all day not to be sad but for about ten minutes I stood at the window and cried. No one knew that I had cried. I stood at the window staring out at the snowflakes slowly falling. They were so gentle and soft looking. I didn't want anyone to know because that would put a damper on everyone's mood. I wondered if every Christmas I would feel a little sad. I knew the answer to that before I even thought about it.

The children started running around in circles when they saw the snow. They wanted to go play in it. Sissy begged me to go with them and how could I pass up an invitation like that. We must have stayed out there for hours because it was really dark when we came in. Our toes were frozen but we didn't care because there was snow for Christmas. Mary Lee had made hot chocolate with marshmallows. We drank our hot chocolate and warmed our toes by the fireplace. The Christmas tree was beautiful as it blinked on and off. I looked around and felt so very content with my little family next to me. As sad as I was hours ago, I felt so happy now.

I began to feel cold feet about moving to South Carolina. I couldn't help but think I had been too impulsive. I went round and round over the question, to move or not to move, as I sat watching the fire long after everyone had gone to bed. I kept thinking about how the house had called me. I could see it in my mind finished. I could see myself sitting on the front porch as the grandchildren played in the yard when they would come to see grandma. I could also see me alone most of the time. No family there, made me feel lonely already.

I, eventually, made myself go to bed. I knew that if I turned it over to God, the answered would come to me. That night, sleep came easy for me. I had been up since before dawn and played in the snow so my body was relieved to climb into bed.

The next morning I moved back to my garage apartment. As soon as I walked into the apartment I knew my answer about moving. I really didn't want to live in a garage apartment in my son's garage for a long time until I move into a nursing home.

I loved being around the children but I knew that I had to find my own place. I felt that I was starting to become my own person. I had been a daughter, sister, wife and mother and now I had to be me. I was a little frightened by all the changes but there was some excitement to facing a new challenge. I was on my way to the beach. What I do after that will be played by ear. The funny thing is I felt absolutely no stress. I have to give my new faith all the credit because it certainly was a new feeling for me.

"As quickly as seasons change, so do our lives."

Chapter 14

Bad Weather - Convincing Weather

The Christmas snow was beautiful but after three days, its beauty turned into brown slush. I couldn't believe that winter had already started, but, in fact, not only had it started but it was on a rampage. The children were thrilled with the snow. They tracked in wet slush all week long. We were constantly washing and drying clothes. Mary Lee was starting to show her pregnancy. I tried to help with the children as much as possible because I could remember being pregnant and so tired. It was a tired like no other. I had even fallen asleep at a stop light once for about a second. I awakened to the person behind me blowing their horn and jolting me awake.

I can't imagine being pregnant four separate times. I wanted more than one child, but I never was able to have more. When I was growing up, I always thought I would have a houseful of little ones, but I wasn't so lucky. Now when I see these children running around I'm not so sure I could have handled it. David worked long hours and I would have had much of the responsibilities. Michael was an easy child but I still fretted over everything. If he had the sniffles I would panic. The good Lord probably knew what he was doing. I find myself a much better grandmother than a mother. Michael always tells me that I am a very good mother though I have my doubts. I know in my heart that there isn't a mother that could love her son as much as I. I find that I love my grandchildren with the very same passion.

I was going to be the official New Year's babysitter. I was trying to think of things I could do with the children to make New Year's Eve exciting for them. The best thing about being a grandmother, is that I can keep them up late, give them lots of sugar, kiss them goodnight and go to my little apartment and Michael and Mary Lee can get them calm after I'm gone. That's just one of the grandmother perks.

New Year's was a blast. I bought a couple bottles of sparkling cider and lots of snacks. We ate most of the night with a few games of Candyland and Go Fish. The girls tried to stay up for the ball to drop, but they fell asleep around ten. Lyle managed to stay up and even kept on having to wake me up. I pretended not to be asleep but I was gone pretty deep. Lyle thought that Dick Clark was my age and that he would be a great new husband for me. I tried to tell him that when I was in middle school, I used to watch him on television. I think he thinks that after you pass thirty you all become the same age. He must think we all become old. I try not to act old but he already has me in that category.

After the holidays were over, the children and Mary Lee went back to school. I continued to work towards my move. I just couldn't set a date. Try as I might, I just couldn't bring myself to put the date on the calendar. I knew that I would know when it was time so I didn't worry about it.

January was such a drab and dreary month; I got so tired of the snow and ice. I just felt that I was too old to trapes around in boots for three months. The children had already had about three snow days. They were getting tired of the weather and so was I.

All I could think about was more snow for February and March. I knew that the sooner I could get to the beach, the sooner that the house could be finished. I wanted the house to be ready for the children's summer vacation. I was hoping that Mary Lee and Michael would let me take them to the beach for a while after the new baby was born. It would be wonderful if I could bring them home with me after I come to help with the baby for a week. Little David was due at the end of June, so the timing would be perfect.

One cold January morning, I woke up to the absence of heat in the apartment. I think that it must have been out for a couple of hours because it was, literally, freezing. I think that was the deciding moment for me. Soon, I would be on my way to Pawley's Island.

I began to pack my things. Michael thought that February first would be an ideal time. He has wanted to go with me and make sure that I get settled somewhere nice while the house is being rebuilt. I would look at all of my traditional furniture and cringe, thinking about it in my little shack. It really wasn't going to fit in. I gave lots of things to Michael and a few select pieces to Joe. I wanted my house to look like me. The me that I have discovered, is different from the me I thought I was supposed to be thirty-five years ago. I was starting a new adventure and I need to leave behind some of my sadness.

Reverend Doss had come by many times to say goodbye. I think he didn't really approve of my leaving but wanted to seem supportive. He has really helped me through such a hard time and I truly have been blessed to have such a wonderful friend. God has led me to follow my heart. What's funny to me, is finally knowing what was in my heart. For so many years, I never thought what made it beat. My goal was always to make David and Michael my priority and I did that very well. I don't resent anything that I did in the past. I do wish I had of told David more that I loved him. I know that he knew, but after he was gone I really didn't think I had said it enough.

I have been in touch with my realtor in South Carolina many times. She had found me a condo to rent by the month until I get Shabby Shack fixed up enough to be able to live there. She had set up interviews with a number of contractors for me. Now that is something I thought that I would never be doing. This should be a real education for me and everyone else involved. Michael wanted to be a part of that but he didn't have the time to stay away from home too long. A part of me was disappointed, but I knew that I had to do this alone. Besides, I know that with my newly found best friend, God, I wouldn't be alone. What a great feeling to have him on my side.

"My God is an Awesome God"

Chapter 15

Back to Comfort

Moving day came. It was a cold, bitter February morning. The movers went through gallons of hot cocoa. We managed to get everything packed up in about five hours. Lyle was not very helpful. He really didn't want me to go so he was major a pain. The girls were fine because they were excited about coming down in June to stay. Of course, they will miss play with me but they have each other for that. Lyle has spent a lot of time with me in the past few months. He told me one day that he was afraid for me to go because he may never see me again. As we talked he told me how much he missed his grandfather. I never realized that David's death had affected Lyle at all until that very moment.

I think that we just tried to pick up where we had left off when it came to the children. Since they never said anything, we never thought about talking to them about how they felt when David died. I guess adults don't think about anything but their own emptiness. We just seem to get consumed in our own grief. I had to reassure Lyle that I would be back every holiday and they would come to the beach more often than just once a year. He seemed to be somewhat happier but still not totally convinced. To him, David had just left without saying goodbye.

As the moving van closed the big doors, I had a sinking feeling. What was I about to do? I thought. Then I felt a real since of calm come over me. I felt as if everything was going to be just fine.

I kissed the children goodbye and told them I would see them in June when baby brother arrived. Mary Lee got a little teary eyed as she hugged me goodbye. I knew she would miss me, but this was an opportunity for them to be a family without my input. Mary Lee had to feel that the house was partially hers as long as I was there. Now she could feel like it was her home. Michael and I got into the car and waved goodbye. As we drove off I felt as if I was a little girl on a new adventure.

It took us forever to get to South Carolina. Michael's car said that he had more gas in it than it did. Just an hour out of town, we ran out of gas. That really got me thinking about omens. I wondered if God was trying to tell me something. When I shared this with Michael, he said that God wasn't saying anything to me but telling him to get his car checked more often. He seemed to be so busy that he never did his regular maintenance.

That was one of the biggest differences in Michael and David. David always had the car checked out before we went anywhere. He was somewhat of a car fanatic. He had his car washed twice a week. Michael is lucky if he gets his car washed once every two months. He ran around with the children in the afternoons. David had me running around with Michael in the afternoons. Michael and Mary Lee have always shared everything fifty, fifty. Michael truly had less time to do things, like wash his car. I guess it boils down to priorities.

A really nice man came by us when we were sitting on the side of the road waiting on AAA. He had gotten gas for his lawn mower and gave us a couple of gallons to get to the next gas station. Funny thing, it was the same gas station that was coming from AAA. They were surprised when we arrived. Who knows when they would have come out because there were only two people manning the station? They didn't seem to be in a big hurry to get anywhere.

It only took us nine hours to get to Pawley's Island. I think that was quicker than the summer trip. Michael seems to take forever traveling. He makes more stops than anyone I know. One thing for sure, you get lots of time to stretch your legs on a trip with him. One would think with only the two of us we would have made record time but that was not the case.

The movers dropped everything off at my storage bin, hours before we had gotten there. I was so glad that my realtor had taken care of everything on that end. We met her at the house I was going to rent until mine was finished. I think I could have stayed at my house but Michael didn't want his mother living in a rundown shack.

Michael stayed a couple of days while I interviewed contractors. What a range of characters. I must have talked with ten people until settling on someone with whom I could work. As soon as a contractor would tell me to tear down the main structure and start over with a new one, I would thank them and send them on their way. Michael, at first, would agree with them but when he finally understood that there was a true connection between the house and me, he was swayed in my direction.

One man drove up in a brand new BMW and was proudly wearing lots of gold jewelry looking like a red neck Godfather. He started talking like I was going to build The Biltmore House. I knew right away he was out of my price range. Some big old guy named Chuck showed up without a shirt on and his big belly hanging over his pants. I'm sure you can picture all of that but don't picture the plumber's crack. I was sure that I couldn't stand looking at him for months. He may have been a great builder, but he was not going to be my builder. I was totally exhausted by the time Darrin DuPuy showed up at the shack. He got out of his Ford truck wearing work boots, jeans and a golf shirt.

I was impressed as soon as he stuck his hand out and introduced himself, first, to me and then Michael. He was truly a southern gentleman. We walked around the property almost silent. I really wanted his take on things before I told him what I wanted. When he looked at me and said, "Mam, I think you have one of the last beauties left on this Island. I hope you won't alter its integrity." Needless to say, I was sold and Michael seemed pleased.

We talked about keeping its natural warmth and making it structurally sound. We seemed to be on the same wave length. Darrin told me his wife had redone an old house recently and that I should talk to her because she was a fount of knowledge in finding salvage that would stay true to the period of the house. I knew that we were not only going to be in business together but we were going to be friends. There was an immediate respect that had developed between the two of us. Darrin told me he could get started right away because he had just finished a job and wasn't going to start another one until June. He said that he was working on his church in his spare time so my house could be his main focus. I truly think it was divine intervention. I felt like God had led me to this person and that I was in capable hands. Looking back on the whole thing, I know that God had his hand on my shoulder leading me to this wonderful family.

It wasn't long before I met his wife Carrie. She was exactly as he had said. We shopped at every antique store and salvage yard from Charleston to Wilmington. I found perfect objects needed to make my little shanty a home.

The renovation wasn't totally smooth. The entire roof had to be replaced. The rafters needed to be reinforced not to mention the floors had termites. Darrin had the floors treated but he thought that some of the damage gave character and I agreed. As long as the termites were gone I was happy. Like most of the houses built in the thirties, the house was only on rock piers. I loved the look, so we shored them up and skirted the foundation with lattice work. The main structure was made out of wood. I think that it had been fifty years since a coat of stain had been applied. Once the grey stain was applied, the house took on a whole new personality. It was no longer a shack, it was a beautiful cottage. The gray cottage needed my personal touch so I shopped for just the right things to put on the front porch.

While shopping with Carrie, I found a wicker settee. We painted it a dark green and I made new cushions for it. She suggested that I add lots of pillows to make it look like an outdoor living room. I sewed for days and made lots of fluffy pillows. She was right because the pillows were perfect for the look of the cottage. I found a really well worn sisal rug and made it fit in front of the settee. Carrie had found a rocker on one of her adventures. She brought it and suggested I paint it red. I wasn't really keen on that idea. I told her I would think about it. So I thought and thought. Red was a little drastic even for the new me. I finally said I would try it and I did. I tried three colors of red until I found just the perfect one called Ruby Lips. I liked it so well that I painted the door red. I had to laugh because I knew David was looking down and thinking that I had completely lost what mind I had left. The color was the new me. I like to tell people it was just a little daring. I think that sums up my new life. We even painted the storm shutters the same soft red. I loved my new house then and I still love it. I felt right at home. Darrin and Carrie came by a lot; even though the house was finished. I started attending their Church. They would come by to get me on Sunday mornings for months. The First United Methodist Church was toward Georgetown so they felt like it was on their way until I was comfortable going on my own. I really did need them at first. I found it scary visiting a new church. I didn't realize how dependent I was on being comfortable in church, sitting with my family. Carrie must have sensed my reluctance in going alone. Now I feel part of the community. I felt as if I had always sat in that pew. It was a warm and comfortable church, one of those that just says welcome sister.

"Ob-La-Di, Ob-La-Da, life goes on."
-The Beatles

Chapter 16

Welcome Hannah

On the right side of the property are many live oaks. Some are small, some look like brush and some are, gracefully, windswept and large. I knew that the property line was shared be my neighbors. I had seen them home a lot lately so I decided to knock on their door and introduce myself and ask it I could have the property line cleaned up and landscaped. Before I could go to their house, Ruth appeared at my door with a beautiful lemon pound cake. She had dressed it with the most scrumptious lemon glaze. When she came inside, she admitted that a part of her visit was out of curiosity. She said that she wanted to meet the person that, finally, had nursed the shanty back to health. I fixed hot jasmine tea and we ate cake. I'm not really sure, but I think that was the first fattening thing I had eaten in months.

Ruth and Bobby Peterson had retired to the Island about four years ago. They had been traveling back and forth to Columbia, South Carolina for a while, but their son bought their house last year so they were going to call this house home, now. I thought they seem very young to be retired. She said Bobby was forty-nine and had been fully retired for two years. He had a small computer business that had grown into a very large business and someone came with the right offer and he jumped on it. Ruth said that she had inherited some property in Charleston but sold it which helped them retire early. She loved being retired and spending time with Bobby. She was one of the cutest girls. You could tell she was very different from me. She was dressed to the nines, her hair was perfect and she wore diamond earrings everyday. Diamonds everyday was a new concept for me. I owned diamond earrings but only wore them on special occasions, occasions that were so special that I never wore them at all. I think that the last time I wore them was on a New Year's Eve, when David took me to the Greenbrier for the Holiday.

That seemed an eternity ago. I felt a sad pang in my heart when I thought of David, especially, when Ruth would talk about spending time with Bobby. I would find my heart crying out for David. I caught myself daydreaming about David and me walking on the beach hand in hand. The old Green Eyed Monster reared its ugly head once again.

Ruth asked me to walk with her in the mornings. I was excited to have a new friend. I had been walking alone and now I would have someone with which to talk. I think that I was most excited to have another new friend. Carrie was really busy helping Darrin with another new house so she had little time. She didn't ever get too busy that she didn't call me every night around seven to share any new finds that she would run across. She was always looking for a great treasurer at a tremendous bargain. We still would do a little shopping but now I had a friend to walk with and keep me in the routine of exercising.

I guess the funny thing is that I never had girl buddies when I was in Virginia. I had my family to occupy most of time. This was really a new thing for me to be sharing my secrets with someone other than my immediate family.

One would think that I would have a hard time adjusting to everything but I seemed to transition with the greatest of ease. Being forced to find out who Hanna Devon Fry was, I was, finally, getting some answers. I know that learning about God's love was the start of my new journey. This was a new life for me. I had always thought that my life was as good as it was ever going to be. I was happy in my little corner, now, I'm finding more joy than I ever thought existed. I wish that David was here to share it with me.

Michael and Mary Lee would call me every Sunday night. They seemed so busy with the girls gymnastics and dancing and Lyle's Scouts and soccer. It was hard to believe that in three months that they would have baby number four. I guess he will be a traveling baby. I had told them that I would come up and help them for a while and bring the children back with me. I still had a few things to get ready in the house before I could have guests. Everyday, I would do a little more on the inside but I had the outside just like I wanted it. Instead of a Shabby Shack, I now had a cozy cottage. Everyone names their house at the Island so I guess that would be my house's name, Cozy Cottage. It was a lot like putting lipstick on a pig. I dressed up Shabby Shack and she became Cozy Cottage.

In March, I met a nice man at the grocery store. I seemed to keep running into him. I was beginning to feel like fate was bringing us together.

I was feeling somewhat like a school girl when I would see him. He eventually asked me out to dinner. I couldn't say no. Really, I couldn't say no because he just wouldn't accept no for an answer.

Maury Jasper picked me up for dinner around seven-thirty one Friday night. He acted a little disappointed that I was ready and waiting on the porch for him. He kept telling me he wanted to see my place. I thought it a little strange he was so interested, but he told me he was thinking about buying a little house like mine and wanted to see how I had finished the floors. I didn't offer for him to come in because I was pretty hungry and a little uncomfortable having a man in my house other than Bobby and Darrin. We went to Georgetown to a little out of the way place on the water. I think that I had three or four glasses of wine. It had been a long time since I had been out with a man and the wine seemed to help my nerves. Now that I look back on it, I think that he was filling my glass every time I turned my head. The more Maury drank, the louder he got. I was ready to go home an hour into the date. In my mind, the date was dead in the water. When we arrived home he ran around the car to help me out. I thought he was just being a gentleman. When we got to the front porch I told him goodnight and fumbled for my keys. Maury kept insisting that he come in for a nightcap. I continued to tell him I was really tired and had a lot to do the following morning. He started pushing his body against mine and started to kiss my neck. I continued to try to push him away but he was too strong for me. The harder I fought him off, the stronger he seemed to get. He grabbed my neck as he started to unzip his pants. I managed to get a weak scream out. I was hoping that someone would hear me.

All of a sudden, someone grabbed him and knocked him down. He was stunned to see a man and his black lab standing on top of him. I realized that it was Bobby. Bobby chased him off and told him that if he ever saw him around here again he would have him arrested. Bobby stayed with me for a while until Ruth could come over. Ruth and Bobby told me I could date no more unless they could pick out the guy. I told them that it was fine by me. I was so upset over what had happened that Ruth stayed with me the rest of the night. I felt so stupid. Was I so lonely for male company that I let my guard down?

Maury seemed quite harmless. I had thought he was such a nice guy. I had lost my good judge of character and my suspicious nature. He must have followed me for a while because he knew way too much about me. While he was trying to get into the house, he kept telling me he knew I needed him because I hadn't been to bed with a man in a year and a half. Somehow he knew personal things about me. I wonder how many other women he had stalked? How many other times had he thought he was servicing women? In his deranged mind he thought he was doing women a favor.

I was so grateful that Bobby and Midnight had been walking. I believe that Maury would have raped me there on the front porch. I lost a lot of my self-assurance for a while until one afternoon Bobby, Ruth and I went up to Windy Hill to shop. Windy Hill is about an hour and half from my house. There in the restaurant was Maury. Bobby went over to speak to him. When he came back to the table he said Maury will never bother me again. I was a little confused. Bobby laughed and told me the woman Maury was with was his wife.

Yes, Maury, sleazebag had a wife. Maury pulled Bobby aside and begged him not to say anything. Bobby told him he wouldn't say anything but he never wanted to see Maury in Pawley's Island again. He warned him he would have charges brought against him, even if he had to make them up. I think Maury was scared to death. His wife looked like a former wrestler and could squish him like a bug. Maybe we somehow had gotten Maury off the prowl. I really doubted it. I feel like Maury was a sexual predator that looked for vulnerable women. In his delusional mind, he thought he was doing women a favor by gracing them with his presence.

I must have been one of his easiest victims. Somehow, he could read on my face just how lonely I was. I said yes way too soon and didn't even know anything about him. I look back and can't believe that my suspicious nature didn't kick in or at least my brain. I knew that I would never make a snap decision concerning men again.

Bobby and Ruth kept insisting that I get a dog. They said it would help me feel secure again. I had never had a dog and didn't think that I wanted one. After they persisted endlessly, I told them I would consider getting a dog but only after the children's visit in the summer.

Much to my surprise, they bought me a dog for an Easter present. He was a big ball of black fluff. Instantly, I fell in love. His face is what charmed me. His eyes were like big brown saucers that looked straight into my heart. His great big paws didn't fit his little body but somehow I knew it wouldn't long before the body would fit the paws. I wanted to pick just the right name. Bobby and Ruth wanted to name him Maury. They said it would be a friendly reminder not to make anymore dating mistakes. I, absolutely, refused to name him Maury. All I wanted to do was to forget that man. I kept thinking of my puppy as my new best friend so I named him Buddy. Buddy was the new male in my life. I really do prefer the four legged males to the two legged ones.

"Dog…A woman's best friend."

Chapter 17

Big Paws and Slobbery Kisses

Buddy was just what the doctor ordered. He was just a great big, black bundle of love. He was unbelievably spastic as he grew into his very large feet. Buddy tripped up and down the steps more than once. He had only one speed, and that was fast.

Buddy wasn't as wild as most puppies. He would even wait patiently for me to fill his bowl with food. He wouldn't even eat until I told him it was alright for him to do so. I had always heard such horror stories about puppies, mostly from my mother, so I didn't know what to expect. I was pleasantly surprised by how easy Buddy and I gained respect for each other.

The only real problem we had was learning to walk together. Buddy didn't take to the leash very well. A lot of our walks would end with me carrying Buddy home. I knew that my back would not last very long doing that. Ruth suggested that we both go to obedience school. I thought that was a great idea. I called a school not far from the island and they had an opening for us. At school Buddy excelled. It wasn't long before he learned to walk on the leash well.

There were a few dogs that weren't quick learners. One boxer named Duke never got the technique. After dragging his owner through a mud puddle, we never saw them again. His owner may still be holding on for dear life. Thank goodness Buddy was a quick study, because this made for much more pleasant walks and saved my back. Ruth said that she enjoyed our walks more but she had less to laugh at. I know that it was a real comedy watching me carry my big dog home. It was either carry him or stay on the beach forever.

Ruth and I walked the dogs every morning. Midnight really liked Buddy. They seemed to be best friends too. We looked forward to our walks and talks together. Since there was no one on the beach this time of year, we would let the dogs run free before heading home. Then we would have to rinse them off before we could let them back into the house. There is nothing like the smell of wet dog but with beach water, combined with sand, it made it all the more offensive. After rinsing both dogs, we had enough sand to make a castle.

At night, Buddy would sit at my feet while I read or watched TV. His was such a great companion for me. Dogs never require much but a friendly word and a pat on the head. Buddy gave me so much more than that. I never knew how much I could love something other than my family but I had a bond with Buddy that goes beyond comprehension.

The temperature was beginning to warm up. I couldn't believe that I had been on the island for over three months. Darrin and Carrie DuPuy were less busy since he had finished the house project down the way and his church he was working on. I had really missed them.

They would come over on Sundays for lunch. I loved entertaining again. Sometimes Ruth and Bobby would come and help with the cooking. Bobby's cooking was hard to beat so I usually let him show off for everyone. Bobby cooked like an Iron Chef. He had a special apron that said "I am the greatest." No one would dispute his abilities. Bobby and Darrin would always retire to the porch after lunch for a beer and cigar while we cleaned the kitchen. I even found dishes fun to do. It was special sharing time with each other. Michael and Mary Lee would call about the time we would be finishing Sunday lunch. They felt as it they already knew everyone. I couldn't wait until they could come down and meet all of my friends and Buddy, too.

The DuPuys fell in love with Buddy. Darrin had wanted a dog ever since his dog died two years before. Darrin had loved that dog as if it were a child. I guess to them it was their child. I used to not understand that kind of attachment but now, since I adopted Buddy, I totally understand. Carrie just wasn't ready to get another dog until she was around Midnight and Buddy. The next thing we knew they had a Golden Retriever. They named him Cuddles. Cuddles was about as hyper as Carrie.

Carrie and Cuddles tried to walk with us in the mornings but Carrie walked too fast for us to keep up. She would be so far ahead of us that sometimes she would be yelling back to us to carry on a conversation. Finally, she realized she wasn't cut out for leisure walks and neither was Cuddles. We would have to settle for our Sunday visits. Carrie and Cuddles were a perfect example of the Energizer Bunny.

I found it so funny that my two best friends were so opposite. Carrie was your basic tree hugger, health nut and Ruth was such a Southern Lady in every since of the word. Here I was right in the middle, I think of myself as little bit of both. I never felt like a fifth wheel with them. Instead, I always felt like I fit right in, just like family.

Buddy proved to be a perfect watch dog. Whenever anyone would come in the yard he would alert me. He made sure people would keep their distance. What was really funny was that he would do the same for Ruth. Buddy adored Bobby and Darrin but wasn't crazy about other men. I don't think he would hurt anyone but I was real careful to keep him in whenever the mailman was around. Uniforms made him a little skidish. I am sleeping so much better now that I had my great protector. I also found myself getting up around five o'clock every morning to let him out. I wasn't accustomed to seeing the sun rise but it was wonderful. I didn't want to miss any of the daylight so I would stay up in the mornings, read the paper and drink my tea for hours. At last, I felt such calmness.

I was thinking of David less but when I did think of him I would really miss his presence in my life. I so wanted to have that feeling of sharing and companionship. The thought of dating again still made me cringe. I didn't want anyone else. I wanted the type of relationship that Ruth and Bobby have. I would even settle for the busy, energized relationship that Darrin and Carrie have.

I was so grateful for every minute spent with Buddy. He was that warm, slobbery part of me that I didn't know I needed. He slept beside my bed every night and by my chair when I sat. I had never, in my life, spent so much time with anything. He was my shadow and I loved him being with me and felt that I would always feel safe with him at my side.

Baby David was getting anxious to make his appearance. Mary Lee had called on Sunday and was starting to dilate. She thought that I needed to be making my plans to come home for a while. They were really surprised that I was going to drive and bring my best friend, Buddy. I was sure that the children would love to help me care for Buddy and get to know him since they were going to come home with me.

The trip back to South Carolina should prove to be very interesting…with one dog and three children and one grandmother. Wow! That's mind boggling. As that famous Southern woman Scarlet O'Hara said," I'll think about that tomorrow."

Ruth had not been able to walk much lately. She was sure that the flu had set in and refused to go. Bobby was walking with us most mornings because Midnight needed the exercise. The funny thing was that when we walked it was like walking with Ruth. Our conversations were as if we picked up from the last walk with Ruth. They had been together so long that they seemed to be one in the same. Bobby was pretty worried about Ruth because she was not one to go to bed, even with a fever. I reassured him that the flu was just hanging around until he got it.

The flu did seem to hang on a long time. Lots of people said it was going around. I was just hoping that it would be gone before the children got down there. It would be awful if they got it while staying with me. That would be a nightmare.

June first came and the weather was perfectly beautiful. The mornings still had a slight coolness but the afternoons were hanging around eighty degrees. I was really surprised to get a call from Michael that afternoon. Baby David had arrived. He was eight pounds five ounces and twenty-two inches long. I packed a few clothes and got Buddy's things together. We were on our way to meet our new member of the family. I knew David must have been looking on with such pleasure. He had left a great legacy.

Traveling with Buddy was really fun. He started out in the back seat but after ten minutes he was riding shot gun. Buddy loved his window cracked so that he could breath the fresh air and snort all over the glass. Buddy became the "King of the Mercedes." I wondered how I was going to get all the kids and Buddy back in my little car. Michael didn't want me to drive. He was hoping he could persuade me to fly but that would mean I would have to put Buddy in the kennel. The thought of that just made me sad. Besides, I wasn't a big fan of flying, I was looking for one more adventure.

While driving to Virginia, I had the brilliant idea to switch cars with Michael. I knew that the children would be happier in the mini-van because they would have their DVD player and there would be plenty of room for kids and dog. The best part would be that Michael would get to drive my car and I am sure that he would love that. They will never own a Mercedes because Mary Lee is much too practical to allow that to happen. Michael would never spend that much money on a car. That's one of the greatest differences between David and Michael. David loved high quality and expensive cars.

I did hope that he wouldn't mind if Buddy slobbered on his windows. I love the old saying, "Love me, Love my dog." Who knows, this may make them want a puppy.

"There's nothing like puppy love!"

Chapter 18

Carry Me Back To Old Virginny

Needless to say everyone was really surprised when Buddy and I arrived. I think Michael was a little annoyed but I'm his mother and he would never say anything. Lyle was the most excited to see me but even more excited to see Buddy. It was love at first sight.

The girls were in love with the new baby. They couldn't do enough for him. He was a beautiful baby. He was almost a pretty as Lyle.

Mary Lee was so happy to see me. She had not had much alone time since David was born. She took lots of time in the shower. I think just to be able to shower and not worry about the children getting into something and the baby not crying was the best part of my visit.

Her parents were coming in a couple of days, so I cleaned everything from stem to stern. Not much had been done for a couple of months. I guess when you are nine months pregnant and three other children housecleaning is not at the top of your priority list, even if it were, you wouldn't feel like cleaning.

Baby David was a noisy little fellow. When he slept, he made a purring sound. The girls said that he sounded like a critter in the house. He was a lucky little boy to have so many people loving him. I loved to hold him. It reminded me of when Michael was little. David thought that I would rub the skin off of him because I would never put him down. Baby David will probably become a little spoiled but why do we have children if we can't spoil them?

After ten days in Virginia I thought it was time for me to go home. I was missing my little cottage and really missing my friends. It was good to see Joe and Sherry. They seemed happier than I had ever seen them before. I really attribute all of his life changes to his finding and embracing God's love. He and Sherry have gotten involved with their youth program at the church. Joe has so much to offer. He would have been a wonderful father had he ever had children. They promised to come down this summer for a long visit. I can't believe that Joe would close the shoe shop for more than a day, but he says that he really is going to take some time off.

Michael packed the car along with Buddy and off we went on our special journey. I hated leaving Baby David but Mary Lee and Michael would have two weeks to bond and cuddle with their new little boy.

It didn't take but thirty minutes for Lyle and Sissy to get in a fight. I really don't know what it was about but I quickly pulled the car over to the side of the road and separated them. Smugly, getting back into the car, I thought that Grandma still had it. No more than twenty minutes passed when Sara wanted to go to the bathroom. When we stopped no one else had to go but I made them get out and try. I walked Buddy, hoping that I would not have to stop, at least for an hour. I was wrong, these children are used to traveling with Michael who stops every twenty minutes. We stopped and stopped and stopped. I finally told everyone that we only had an hour left and we were not going to stop anymore. I held to my promise and no one even asked or maybe they were afraid to ask this grumpy old lady.

It was almost dark when we got to Pawley's. The children wanted to go to the beach. I quickly unpacked the car and got Buddy's leash and we ran to the beach for about thirty minutes. When we got back to the house Darrin and Carrie were there with pizza. I was so glad to see them. And Buddy was really happy to see that over active Cuddles. The dogs got the children really hyper and I knew that they would never go to bed. I was right. After the DuPuys left, they were still wide open. I was so exhausted that I fixed warm milk that Carrie had brought and read a couple of stories. Around eleven, they finally dosed off. When I got into my bed, I smiled with pride. I was so grateful for that day. It was filled with tension, fussing, a few tears, lots of smiling and singing but most of all it was filled with love. God has truly given me so many blessings. It took me a long time to recognize his gifts but I can see his constant love and care for me.

The children kept me busy every minute of the day. We played hard. Lyle fell deeply in love with Buddy. I was really afraid that he would find it hard to leave and go back home. Maybe Mary Lee would break down and let Lyle get his own dog. I know that it would make it a lot easier for him to go back home. You always hear stories about boys and their dogs and this is no exception. Their bond was instant. I would find Lyle on the floor sleeping with Buddy most every morning. Even though Lyle is ten, I think the new baby has created a little insecurity. Maybe a new dog for him would be the right thing.

I have seen very little of Bobby and Ruth. She was still feeling as if she had the flu. Bobby seemed to be really worried and had tried to get her to go to the doctor but she kept insisting that she was feeling better. She looked really weak and seemed to be so thin. It had been four weeks since she had gotten the flu. She said she hated to go to the doctor and hated to be told what she already knew. I could sympathize with her. Some doctors made you feel like a hypochondriac.

I wasn't sure what Bobby and Ruth had been eating so I made my famous spaghetti and took some over to them. The children ate so much that I was afraid that they would be sick but an hour later they wanted ice cream. I remember the days when I couldn't get filled but now I eat about half what Lyle eats. I don't know where he puts it. He eats as if he has a hollow leg.

The girls love the shopping trips and Lyle loved the beach. I think his favorite part was playing in the surf with Buddy. There is nothing worse than wet dog but wet dog and wet boy was a combination that I was totally unfamiliar with. Thank goodness for my outside shower so they could leave their fragrances in the yard.

Every afternoon I would talk the children into sitting in the swing on the porch and reading. I needed the down time. I was so worn out about mid-afternoon that all I could think of was a cup of hot tea and to put my feet up.

Lyle and Sissy explored every corner of my lot. They found rocks, shells and lizards. Sara didn't share their love of exploration. She wanted to read or knit. I had shown her what I knew about knitting, which wasn't very much. I knew just enough to get her going. The bug had bitten her. She was totally "hooked" and wanted to chain stitch all day. She really seemed to have my genes. She had about the same energy level that I have. Sara and I were perfectly happy sitting on the porch knitting or reading a good book.

The children's visit was much too short but they were all enrolled in camp the following week. I really think they would have rather stayed here with their granny.

Michael came for such a short visit. I hardly had time to say hello and then I was waving goodbye. I knew I was going to miss my babies a lot. The truth be known, I think Buddy was going to miss all the attention Lyle gave him. In such a short time, they had made a permanent bond.

It had been days since I had seen Ruth. She was still not feeling well and I was really beginning to worry. Bobby had been taking care of her for over six weeks. The strain of worry was beginning to show on his face.

"Catch and Release"

Chapter 19

Where are you, God?

I wondered if I should tell Bobby just how concerned I was. I only knew she had to see a doctor. I felt as if she sensed something was seriously wrong. Ruth just seemed to get worse day by day. She wasn't eating or drinking as much as she should. Sleep seemed to totally overtake her days. Ruth, finally, agreed to see a doctor the next day.

That evening Bobby came running over to the house, He didn't knock but burst in, obviously in a panic. Completely breathless, he told me he couldn't awaken Ruth. He just kept telling me she was totally limp, limp as a dishrag.

I was already in my nightgown though it was only eight o'clock. Exhaustion had taken over after the children's visit and climbing into bed was all the energy that I had left. I probably was suffering from let down after their leaving, though at that very moment, sleep was all I could think about.

Without a thought, I ran with Bobby to Ruth's bedroom. She was barely conscious when we knelt beside her. I was paralyzed by fear. She could barely moan. I grabbed her hand and she asked for help. I reassured her that help was on the way. Bobby had called 911. In the distance I could hear the whine of the sirens.

All I could think of was to pray. I just kept asking God to take care of my friend. I wanted to grow old living next door to her. I wanted to share recipes with her and borrow a cup of sugar. Although we had only been friends for a couple of months, I felt her life was so important to mine. Our connection was instant and I was not about to give my best friend up.

Bobby and I arrived at the emergency room seconds after the ambulance arrived. As they wheeled her into the building she looked as if she were a small child. Ruth was a little person to begin with, but since she had been sick, she was emaciated looking. Her weight loss must have been enormous. She was seriously ill and for some reason she hadn't wanted to see a doctor. I just couldn't understand why she hadn't seen a doctor because she was such a smart person.

Bobby paced back and forth. No one would give him more information other than she was being stabilized. The emergency room doctor was trying to reach her oncologist. The word Oncologist almost went over my head. What's this about an Oncologist? She had not mentioned Cancer before.

I had grabbed a robe on the way out of my door but my feet were bare. I guess from nerves, I was freezing. It was about eighty-five degrees outside but inside the hospital it seemed like it was forty degrees. Bobby was still in his yesterday clothes. He had spilled something on the front of him and looked totally disheveled. I had noticed that lately he wasn't as particular in his appearance as he had been before. I could completely understand that, because he had been consumed with worry.

After eight hours, a doctor came out to talk with us. He had a lot to say some of which I didn't understand and some things I didn't want to hear. The one word he said that rang out over and over in my head was cancer. Bobby sat in silence for a few minutes and then buried his head in his lap and said over and over, no. Not again!

The doctor told us a lot of which we didn't understand but somewhere in the conversation he told us Ruth had been to see her oncologist some months ago. Her doctor had then told her that her cancer had returned. It had been twelve years since she had breast cancer. She was sure she had beaten it, but when she began to feel so badly she had made an appointment, only to find her cancer had returned with a vengeance.

Ruth had known this for a year. She had chosen not to tell Bobby. She had wanted their last months together to be happy times. When she had gotten so sick some six or eight weeks ago she really thought that she had the flu but that wasn't the case. She had always been a strong faithful woman and she wanted to fight the cancer to the end and she had done just that. Though she put up a great fight, her adversary was much too strong for her fragile little body.

Bobby just cried for a long time and all I could do was to pat his back and try to console him. Finally, they came to get Bobby to go up stairs to her room where he could see her. He asked if I wanted to go but I thought that this was a personal time for them so I stayed behind. I really did want to go but knew that it was not my time to be consoled. I would have some time with her later, after Bobby could come to grips with this awful news. In a way, I knew what he was going through. He at least was going to get to say goodbye, I never got that opportunity. I quickly erased all of my selfish thoughts and prayed that God's will be done and I knew that it would.

The next day, I got to go in and see my new best friend. There were many tubes in her, yet she managed to smile and reach her hand out to me. As I sat and held her hand, I started to think back on our last few walks on the beach.

I remembered she talked much more seriously the last few times we walked than ever before. I just thought that she was feeling more comfortable in our relationship that she could open up more. She was noticing the smallest of things and their details. At one time, she grabbed my hand as we walked. It seemed as if she never wanted to let go. I quizzed her a couple of times because I was feeling as if she wanted to tell me something. She always said no that she only wanted to take in every moment that she could. I would have never guessed anything bad was about to happen to her because she had a childlike excitement about life as if she was experiencing it for the first time. It never occurred to me that she was dying. I'm sure that was her plan. She was sparing us worrying and months of sadness that she had kept it all inside. Her strength and faith in God awed me.

After a week in the hospital, she insisted that she go home. For the next five weeks, I sat by her side. She was very weak but still had her sense of humor. Many days she would want me to write down her thoughts. I would try to tell her she was going to be fine and she would soon be able to write her thoughts herself. I knew deep inside that she wasn't going to beat this insidious disease. I tried to keep up a good front but I have never been a good liar and she knew that.

One day, Ruth shared her faith with me. She reassured me that she wasn't afraid to die. The only thing she was afraid of was how Bobby would take it. Ruth worried a lot about him because she didn't think his faith was as strong as it should be. She knew that he would miss her and was afraid that he would just never be able to heal from his pain of loosing her. Ruth shared with me that everyone always thought of Bobby as the strong one, but she felt as if she was the glue that held everything together. Bobby had wrapped his life around their life together.

I was so surprised to hear her talked like that because I had always thought of Bobby as a very strong person. As I observed him the following weeks, I saw exactly what she was talking about. He just seemed to come unraveled. I wanted to be able to help, but I didn't know how to approach him and so I chose not to because he would either be crying or ranting in anger. He wasn't able to accept the fact that Ruth was dying.

I wished that I shared Ruth's total faith in God. I wasn't so sure of my final destination. She was very secure that she would go to Heaven and seem at peace with her finality on earth.

Ruth wanted to write letters to several people, so I wrote the words as she dictated to me. I felt as if I was as close to her as a sister. Ruth wrote letters to her two brothers. She told them how lucky she felt to have them in her life. She told them of her great love for them and her family. She wrote many funny things about their growing up in a small rural area outside of Columbia, South Carolina. We laughed about the crazy things that her brothers did to her. They sabotaged every date she had because they didn't think anyone was good enough for their little sister. It wasn't until she went to college that they were unable to spy on her dates and run off some unexpecting suitor. Ruth said that when she started dating Bobby, she kept it a secret because she was afraid they would run him off. When they finally met Bobby, they loved him.

Ruth wrote a beautiful letter to her son William. Her pride in him could be seen in every line she wrote. She shared her love and pride in words that were so beautifully constructed that they sounded like music. Ruth carefully crafted her words so not to be sad but profound. She painted a beautiful picture of a mother's love. William would be able to hold on to her memory forever by reading her love letter.

Her letter to Bobby was the hardest for her to write. As she spoke, I wrote. We cried together many times. Her love for him was so incredible. It was magical. What they shared was a lot like what I felt David and I shared, though I didn't tell David enough how much I loved him. Writing Ruth's letter to Bobby brought back old feelings. There were times that I felt as if I would drown in my tears but I would have to reach deep inside so that I could be strong for my dear, sweet friend. I could feel the sting of tears swell inside of me and then I would have to swallow my personal pain and be strong for Ruth. She felt lucky that she was able to write letters to her loved ones. She wanted to able to say goodbye to each one of them in a very special and unique way. When it came to Bobby, she was afraid that his grief would smother him and I was beginning to think that it was going to happen, as well.

Ruth didn't know how angry I was feeling that my little friend was slipping away. One morning, she did tell me not to blame God for my misfortunes, but thank him for my experiences. She told me that our experiences make us who we are and without these experiences we would be someone totally different. She was right. I didn't want to be anyone else because I wouldn't have known all the special people that have crossed my life and made it better. She made me promise that I would turn to God for strength and rely on him alone to get me through. I promised her because for some reason so many God-like people had been put into my life and I was going to find out why.

Bobby and I took turns reading to her. She loved hearing over and over the twenty-third Psalm. As she became weaker we would just sit and read to her hours on end. She had gotten too weak to dictate to me by this time. Her face would show her pleasure in the words of the Bible. As I read to her, I found great consolation for myself. One night, Ruth was able to quietly speak to me and said that she would be watching me with David and that I better behave. We laughed together until she had to sleep. Her smile never left her face that afternoon.

Her pain had become more than she could handle so Bobby told her that he was going to call Hospice in to help her be more comfortable. She didn't want to go on strong medication because she wanted to be aware of everything. Bobby made the call anyway because he couldn't bear to see her pain.

Ruth's determination overcame any thought of Hospice. She closed her eyes that evening and passed away. She did it her way. Ruth's strength was present until her last breath. She overcame her pain by leaving it behind.

Ruth had asked me to sing at her funeral. She wanted me to sing her favorite hymn. I wasn't familiar with it though it had been in the Methodist hymnal for some time but when I heard it I knew why she wanted it sung. As I sung "Lord, You have come to the lakeshore" I felt her presence standing beside me. As I sang the refrain for the last time my voice quivered. I reached deep inside for enough voice to finish the song Ruth had come to God's Lakeshore and she was home. The words of the refrain are so very powerful and so befitting for Ruth, "O Lord, with your eyes you have searched me and while smiling have spoken my name. Now, my boat's left on the shoreline behind me, by your side, I will seek other shores." The tears were streaming down my cheeks. The sting of grief burned within me but somehow the words of the song pulled me through.

The funeral was held in Columbia, South Carolina at College Place United Methodist Church. Ruth was a graduate of Columbia College. Columbia College is a small women's college located by the church. The college was so lovely. It just fit Ruth's persona. She and Bobby had been married in the historic church. Their house which they had sold to their son was not far from there. After the funeral we went to the house on Confederate Street. It was an old house that they had refurbished. It was very different from the house at the beach. It looked like a jeweled southern lady. Since William had bought the house from them he had made very few changes because he felt his mother had caught the essence of the old painted lady perfectly.

Lunch was beautifully prepared. We sat for a couple of hours talking about Ruth. Her brothers thanked me for helping her with the letters because it meant so much to them to have her words to comfort them.

It was getting late, so I started to excuse myself in order to drive home before the sun set. It was about two or so hours to Pawley's Island. Carrie and Darrin were keeping Buddy. William insisted that I not leave but stay at the house for the night. I was relieved because I was totally drained from the day.

I left early the next day because I was missing my dog, Buddy. I didn't even bother with eating breakfast. I just needed to see my dog. Bobby stayed in Columbia. He seemed so lost. I remembered that feeling oh so well. It is a numb and surreal feeling. Words can't describe the deep void you are suddenly faced to endure.

August was at an end. Summer was about gone, although summer leaves later in South Carolina than it does in Virginia. It had really been lonely not seeing lights next door. I was so sad not to see Midnight running about, when I would drive into the driveway. Buddy even seemed to sense the change. I knew he missed running with Midnight on the beach though we had not done so in months. I believe that Buddy missed Midnight as much as I missed Ruth. I had missed our walks on the beach. I longed for one more walk with her. I knew that that wasn't going to happen. I remembered how many times I had wished for one more day with David and it never came.

I grabbed Buddy's leash and we went for a walk for hours. We walked so long that it was hard for us to get home. Both Buddy and I were not used to walking without Ruth and Midnight. The truth was that we needed to get back into shape.

A week later, Bobby and William came back to the island. They stayed to themselves for days. I could see the lights on and off but I left them alone to sort out their pain. One morning, they came over for a cup of coffee. I sensed they wanted to talk. Finally, after polite conversation Bobby told me he was moving back to Columbia and selling the beach house. I was stunned, though I knew that something like this could happen. I just didn't believe that it would. My heart felt heavy but I did understand.

Bobby felt a need to explain his decision. He told me that Ruth wanted to move to the beach so that he would take more time away from work and spend more time together as a couple. Either she knew then she was dying or maybe just sensed something no one else would have understood. She did seem to have a direct line to Heaven.

William wanted him to move into the house with him but Bobby had bought a condominium about a block from his office. I could see him getting back into his business and burying himself in work.

After they had broken the news, they quickly left. I wished them well but deep down I was crushed. It was as if nothing that had happened before ever existed. My friends were leaving me behind. I knew I was being selfish but at that time I didn't care. I knew I was wrong to feel hurt but changing that fact wasn't going to happen. I felt abandoned.

When they left I went over and sat on the floor by Buddy. He licked me in the face and then put his head in my lap. Somehow that made me feel a lot better.

I called Michael and Mary Lee just to hear their voices. I needed them to make me feel better. I suddenly was missing them so much and thought about a quick trip home.

"Sometimes people pass through our lives all too quickly."

Chapter 20

September Changes

After three weeks on the market, Ruth and Bobby's house sold. I got really excited because I was so tired of seeing it dark. I missed the lights, I missed Ruth and Bobby, and I missed Midnight. I loved his spastic trot. Whenever I would drive up my driveway, he would lope over to greet me but he was most excited to see his friend, Buddy. I hated the fact that I would never see him and Ruth again. I had gotten used to not seeing much of Bobby. Ever since that night Ruth was rushed to the hospital, he had made himself very scarce.

Darrin and Carrie had been wonderful about keeping me busy. I had them over to eat a couple of times a week. I loved their company. Carrie could make anyone feel great. She has a funny and blunt way of looking at life. Her take on everything is special and unique to her.

The day after Ruth's house sold, I invited Darrin and Carrie for dinner. I needed to see a friendly face and share conversation with someone other than Buddy. Darrin was the grill master, and if you didn't believe him he would prove to you his title was legitimate. He could make shoe leather taste like melt in your mouth t-bone steaks.

They showed up with beautiful filets and the largest potatoes I had ever seen. They knew I needed to eat, drink and try to be merry. I made my Chocolate Tipsy cake. I had soaked it in a cup of bourbon, a made a warm chocolate sauce to pour over the top, and maybe if we were feeling like living on the edge I would add a little vanilla ice cream.

Needless to say, we ate ourselves into a coma. It was the most pleasant feeling of full that I had ever experienced. I even had to loosen my belt and I'm not sure, but I think I drooled a little.

Wherever Darrin went, Cuddles was close behind. What a pair they made. Darrin, a big old southern, country boy and his best friend Cuddles, a clumsy ball of fluff. Both had a lumber to their gait and a gentle nature.

Carrie felt somewhat left out, so she bought herself a tiny little dog. I think she said it was a Cavalier. Her dog looked like a miniature Springer Spaniel to me. Carrie named him Eli. Naturally, when they came for dinner they brought their babies. Buddy was always happy to see them. Our dogs were just part of our family. I look back on all the time I spent without a dog and think what a tremendous loss that was.

Darrin came in and immediately started talking about how disappointed he was in the sale of Bobby's house. I had no idea what he was talking about. He, obviously, thought I knew what was going on. I asked him what he meant by being disappointed by the sale of Ruth's house.

He then told me that the man that bought the house owned four other houses on the Island and rented them out. He was known to let his property deteriorate quickly. It felt as if I had been stabbed in the back. I completely fell apart. Darrin felt so badly for blurting out his news. He thought that Bobby would have told me. He didn't know that Bobby had not spoken to me since he told me that he was selling the house. I told Darrin it wasn't his fault and that I would have found out sometime and that I refused to allow the news to ruin our night though I knew it already had.

The rest of the night, I acted as if what ever happened next door didn't matter. I threw up my hands and I told them life goes on. I needed some way to deal with the bad news. I was such a liar. I was devastated over the thought of having a rental property beside my shabby little cottage. I was losing that wonderful secure feeling that I once had. I think the real emotion I was feeling was anger. It was as if Bobby didn't care what I felt about anything. I thought we were friends but I didn't feel like I had meant anything to him at that moment. Ruth was right, she was the glue and I think the brains. He had lost all sense of reality.

If it had not been for Carrie and Darrin, I think I would have been the loneliest person on earth. Of course, Buddy was really my saving grace. He knew what to do when I was sad. It amazes me how he sensed my emotions. I loved the fact he thought of himself as a lapdog, all 110 pounds.

Toward the end of September the first group of renters moved in. They were down to take advantage of all the golf packages. The area had so many golf courses that they competed with each other by offering deals to play their course. It was a good deal if you were a golfer, but it wasn't a good deal for the home owners. These people would come down and take over our little community. The economy was diffidently reflected by the influx of Snow Birds or northern golfers.

These were not your typical golfers. I believed that beer drinking and gentlemen's clubs were at the top of their list of things to do. I'm sure that they told their wives they were coming for the golf but I knew better.

The weather was perfect all fall. When the renters would arrive home at two in the morning, they would go out in back of the house and play drinking games. They were loud and obnoxious. Four-letter words flew around like the mosquitoes that plagued the coast. How could they stay up all night drinking and manage to play golf the next day?

Buddy was going crazy that first night they arrived. Their shenanigans continued for days. Finally, after the fourth night I called the police because they had moved their party into my back yard. The Island police don't take kindly to strangers disrupting the locals. In the wink of an eye, they had chased them back to their house and things got a lot quieter for the rest of the week. I was so glad when Saturday arrived and they went home.

I was happy to have Buddy because, I knew after the way he had behaved when the renters decided to party at my house, he would protect me. Buddy stayed by my side constantly, fur raised and a low, deep growl every time he heard the next door neighbors…excuse me, party animals too close to the house.

No sooner did those guys leave that another group arrived and another group and another. The chaos was getting to me. Some of the renters where quiet and some of them were not so quiet. It seemed the loud ones out-numbered the quiet ones. Many came for the love of the sport and others came for no apparent reason but to party hard. I had always heard that golf was a gentleman's game. Somehow, that had not been conveyed to most of these people. I like to have fun like the next guy but this was way over the top. Buddy stayed on the edge, truthfully speaking, so did I.

As October arrived, the golf season was at its peak and I was quickly losing my enthusiasm for this area. The anniversary of David's death was upon us. It had been two years. Two years isn't such a long time but to me it seemed to be an eternity. Michael and his family were coming that week to spend some family time with me. The year before, we had a huge party. This year was going to be different; it was going to be a family event. We would celebrate his life quietly, but, none the less, we would celebrate. Although Darrin and Carrie didn't know David, I had invited them to come for dinner. They had become my family away from home and I was excited for both of my families to meet.

Michael had taken the children out of school for a week. He felt that as a family we needed to be together. I had suggested that I would go to Virginia but he wanted to take some time off work and he knew if he came to Pawley's that he could completely relax.

They were going to stay through Halloween. The girls were afraid that we didn't have trick or treating on the Island but I assured them that we most certainly did and they would get lots of candy. I hoped that I was right because I really hadn't gotten to know many of my neighbors. Most of my neighbors had children and were much younger than I, so I had never thought that we would have anything in common. I was hoping that Halloween was a part of life on the Island. Lyle was beginning to think he was too old to trick or treat, so it didn't matter to him one way or the other.

My family meant so much to me this time of the year. They were always important but I just wanted to be surrounded by my loved ones. I was really missing my grandchildren. I was so far removed from baby David. I was missing all the baby things that babies do. He wasn't going to know his grandmother and I hated to think about that.

Lyle was ten and a half. I couldn't believe he was getting so old. He and I had always had a special relationship. I wanted Lyle and my relationship to stay as it was and the miles weren't going to change that.

I was beginning to doubt my decision to move from Virginia. I loved it here but I loved Virginia too. What was I trying to accomplish by moving? I kept thinking about that for days. Had I made a mistake or was I temporarily insane? I had spread my wings but I had run into a head wind. That head wind was probably losing Ruth, and Bobby selling the house.

The family arrived about three hours later than expected. Mary Lee was about out of patience. She had never been much of a traveler and with four children and Michael, she will be even less of a traveler. Michael, as I have said many times, is the world's worse traveler. He stops every twenty minutes. Mary Lee said that he blamed the children for many of his stops but we both knew better. Fortunately, the baby had slept most of the way. He was now almost five months old. Mary Lee was still nursing so she was pretty miserable. After nine hours of not nursing, all she could think about was running to the back to feed him. She could hardly say hello. She ran straight to the back bedroom to feed David. The baby was so hungry that he was trying to eat too fast. I didn't know who was more frustrated, engorged Mary Lee or starving Baby David. Michael wanted to help but soon appeared in the kitchen throwing his arms in the air. I think he must have been making things worse and I also think Mary Lee was rather agitated over their long trip. The last thing she needed was Michael trying to help her nurse the baby. After a most painful nursing session and a small glass of Shiraz, Mary Lee was back to her sweet, patient self. I'm so glad to have us all together. I was feeling a great sense of completeness.

Lyle was really happy to see Buddy and Buddy was happier to see Lyle. They were rolling all over the floor. The girls were sitting almost on top of me. I knew I truly had been missed.

Darrin, Carrie, Cuddles and Eli arrived shortly after Michael. Darrin brought over more big steaks, which resembled roasts, for grilling. Three dogs, five adults and four children crammed into my shabby little cottage made for close quarters. None the less, it was most satisfying. I just wanted to wrap my arms around the night.

Close to midnight, we all found a place to sleep. Michael, Mary Lee and the baby found their way to my extra bedroom while Lyle put a sleeping bag on the floor right next to Buddy. The girls crawled into my bed one on either side of me. After having lots of wine and laughing through the evening, Darrin and Carrie thought it safer to stay the night so they pulled out the sofa bed in the living room. Cuddles and Eli jumped into the bed with their owners and I made my way to my spot in my bed.

What a night! As I crawled into the bed I felt myself smile not a grin but a wide toothed, big smile. That was the first time in a long time I think I was truly happy.

After David died, I found myself sort of wandering aimlessly. I had not thought I was wandering until that night. I had to do something with my life. I had to give back something because I truly felt God had blessed me with a wonderful family and truly great friends. I prayed that night that God would show me just what he wanted me to do with my life. I wanted to be the kind of person that lives by blind faith. I wanted to be a person that could totally turn their life over to God and then not worry about it. I had never been that kind of person before and I had my doubts that I could be now but I was willing to try.

I wondered why God had put so many strong people in my life. He had given me my father. I never thought of my father as a strong person when I was growing up but he must have been to have stayed with my mother all those years. My father had given Joe and me stability. We always knew he loved us and was there for us. Then there was David, who had taken wonderful care of me for all of those years. His strength and faith were unshakable. Of course, there are Michael and Mary Lee whom I admire so very much. They are so young but so strong and noble. Then He put Ruth into my life for some reason, though, she was only in my life for such a short time. She had made a great impact on my heart. As I watched her slip away, she never gave up her love of God. She seemed to know Him so much more than I felt I could ever know Him. She was confident that she would be in Heaven. She never doubted that her Heavenly Father would come for her. Toward the end of her life, when she would grab my hand, I would feel something special running through her and into me. I even mentioned it to her once and she assured me it was the Holy Spirit. I almost laughed when she told me that but I realized that she meant it. It was nothing that I had felt before and I knew it was special. I wondered why The Holy Spirit would run through me or even why it would want too. But that night, with my family nearby, after we all went to bed I felt the Spirit. I knew that God was present in my life. I knew that I wanted what Ruth had. I wanted to be sure, I wanted to feel God with me all of my life. I wanted to go to Heaven so I was prepared to do whatever God wanted me to do or go where ever He wanted me to go.

"Home is where the heart is."

Chapter 21

Home Sweet Home

I decided to tell Michael about doubting my decision to move to the Island. His reaction wasn't at all what I expected. He seemed to be glad that I had done something on my own by moving away. He felt that I had grown in my faith and in my emotions during the time I had been gone. He was right; I had grown in a lot of ways. I wasn't the same woman who had moved to the Island almost a year ago. I was surer of myself and who Hanna Fry was becoming. Even though I was starting to think I had made the wrong decision to move, Michael didn't share my feelings that I had made a mistake. Michael thought I needed the time to think without the pressures of family or the memory of David all around me.

I told him how worried that I was about not watching the children grow. We talked about the fact that I didn't want to miss the baby's first steps or his first words. I asked him if he thought I should move home. It's funny how we make decisions for our children when they are young and then the table turns and they help us with our decisions.

Michael said that I needed time to think and process all of this. I wanted him to tell me what to do but he was right. I sat and listened as he threw out a few options for me to consider. When he said that he thought I needed to keep my cottage and winter here because of the warmer weather I totally thought that sounded reasonable. I really hated ice and snow. Not really hated it but hated the fact that it was confining. I guess two houses wouldn't be awful. Michael wanted to pay for an addition to the cottage. He thought that an extra bedroom and a bigger bathroom would be perfect when the entire family would come to visit. I was really excited about all of our plans.

We called Darrin to discuss the addition the very next day. Naturally, Darrin thought it was a fantastic idea. He told me that it would be in keeping with the area and it could only increase my property value. I found that amusing because the realtor didn't even want me to look at the place. She was convinced it was beyond repair and could never be reborn. I guess we showed her and everyone else.

It was settled, I would stay here for the renovations and the family would come back for a two week vacation in June. Michael would come down the second week because he didn't think that he could take off from work for two weeks. As much as I wanted to see him, I was looking forward to spending a week alone with Mary Lee. I loved her company and I really felt as if she were my own daughter. I admired her for so many things but most of all I admired ability to absorb life with a smile.

It didn't take Darrin long to come back with drawings of his proposed addition. It was lovely. He had taken the liberty to add a tower on top with a spiral staircase to ascend to the tip of the roof where a balcony would sit above the trees. Of course, it couldn't be too tall because of restrictions on the Island. He had great vision and I had total trust in him.

By the middle of November, he had started putting in the walls. It was really taking up a lot of my yard but that only meant less grass and that pleased me. The grass there was pretty sparse so this was a huge improvement. Plus, it was less yard for me to take care of and we all know I don't have a green thumb.

Darrin and Carrie decided to set me up with Darrin's brother because he was coming in for Thanksgiving. I had decided to stay for Thanksgiving since I was going home for Christmas. Besides, I had an addition to build. Darrin's brother, Dallas, had been divorced for about four years. He had dated some but found it difficult. He had been devastated by his divorce and had buried himself into his work. Both of us were pretty reluctant at first because I think that we are both pretty shy people.

Dallas is a Patent Lawyer. I have no idea what a patent lawyer is but that would be a good conversation point. I was excited about the prospect of dating again but a little hesitant. I was hoping that this time it would be better than the date with Maury. I really don't think it could be any worse. Besides, I had Darrin and Carrie with me. A double date was the way to go. I told Darrin if the date turned out badly that my addition to the cottage would be free. He laughed and told me that if his brother didn't have fun he would put my windows in sideways.

The day finally arrived for my date. I was a little nervous but excited at the same time. Dallas was going to come to pick me up but he brought some little sports car and I couldn't get Buddy into it. Carrie had failed to tell him that we go nowhere without our dogs. I was happy to drive over to Carrie's house so that I could bring my dog and leave if things were not going well. Bringing my dog would be a true test of whether we should ever go out again. Looking for a relationship wasn't the reason I was going. I just wanted to feel like a desirable woman again. I had missed getting dolled up with make-up and jewelry and yes, trying to impress a man. Dolled up for me was shaving my legs and putting on lipstick and maybe my diamond earrings.

Carrie and I had been cooking for days. We had made all of the traditional Thanksgiving dishes and then some. It was a huge feast. The turkey was perfectly golden brown and the smells were intoxicating. The yeast rolls were dripping with country butter and the mashed potatoes were swimming in giblet gravy. The calories were jumping out at us but we didn't care because we were hypnotized by the fragrances.

When I met Dallas, I was very surprised. He wasn't as tall as Darrin and not as heavy. Dallas was in perfect shape. He really looked as if he had stepped off of a magazine cover. He was quiet like Darrin and when he spoke he had the same inflection in his voice. He had dark hair and Darrin had blonde. They really didn't look like brothers but when they began to tell old stories of growing up, I saw the brotherly connection. Their manners were perfect and they were very respectful of women. Both Darrin and Dallas had true southern manners when it came to women. I found myself getting a little giddy when he would talk to me. Maybe it was the wine, I don't know. Dallas and I hit it off pretty well that day. I even got a kiss before I left though it was only on the cheek it was affection. How I had longed for that.

We went out a few more times before he left for Atlanta. Most of the time, we took Buddy because Dallas really liked dogs. Though I had only met him a few days before I was going to miss his company. This was new for me and I was enjoying every minute. Dallas no sooner arrived in Atlanta that he called me to tell me how much fun he had over the last few days. We continued to call each other and kept our e-mail hot for the next few weeks. Where this would go was a mystery to me but I was having fun and I liked that.

I was still struggling with the thought of giving back something of me. I hadn't gotten a message from God as to where I could do some kind of community service or something that would help people. Maybe I had gotten the message I just didn't listen. I was new to this trusting God thing.

I talked with my minister and he suggested that I go to Alcoholics Anonymous and listen to some of their stories. I had been sharing some of my past with him and found that he was a great source of compassion. I felt funny going to an AA meeting but took his suggestion. I didn't want anyone to think I was an alcoholic. How silly that was because there were all sorts of people there. Some had suffered from the disease and some had suffered because of the disease. I realized that I was in the latter group. I didn't say anything that first night. I just listened. I was mesmerized by their stories. Some of the stories were just like mine. I had truly suffered from the affect of my mother's disease. I continued to go for a few weeks. It came to me that maybe I needed to share my story. I was thinking that maybe by telling my story I would be able to let go of the past and help someone else at the same time. Like Ruth said one time," Your experiences make you who you are." I am Hanna Devon Fry, a child of an alcoholic. That's who I am and who I will always be. It is up to me to be a good person or not. It is no one's fault but my own if I continue to be a victim.

I asked my minister if I could speak about this some Sunday during Church and he thought that was a wonderful idea. He immediately got out his calendar and set a date. He didn't give me a chance to back out.

I struggled as I wrote my message. I found myself wanting to leave out so many important things. I was too embarrassed to mention some of the things that my mother had done. I tried to bargain with God. I would leave out some things and He would steer me back down the right path. I'm sure he was saying, "No Hanna you need to tell it all." I thought I could tell part of the story but I found out differently.

The Sunday Service came quickly for me to speak. The days leading up to my talk had turned into minutes. I thought that I had written a pretty powerful message. I was confident that I would do well because I had asked God to help me get through this. The time was now and there was no turning back.

As it became my time to speak I walked to the pulpit. A nervous feeling in the pit of my stomach began to boil. When I looked out and saw that Dallas had come to hear me speak. I felt very nervous and was quite surprised. What was he going to think of me and how I was reared? It certainly was very different from his up bringing. I thought about soft stepping my life but what good would that do? God had wanted me to do this and he wanted me to do it His way. I know that because it turned out very differently from how I had planned.

I began by telling everyone about my father and how much I loved him and looked up to him. I talked about my brother Joe and how close Joe and I are. Then it was time to talk about my mother.

I started by saying, "My mother was a mean spirited women. I don't think that she had always been that way because I knew that my father would not have made the mistake of marrying her. Something happened to make her so angry and it will always remain a mystery. My mother was just a miserable soul. She always wanted what other people had and if she couldn't have it she would go into a tail spin. Her screams could be heard for miles. My father was a shoe repairman. We didn't have a lot of money and she brought that up all the time. She was jealous when my father would buy us school supplies because that was money she couldn't have to spend on alcohol. She drank to forget and she drank to remember. She really didn't need a reason.

I could always tell when she had been drinking which was most of the time because her face actually looked different. She would get a hateful look and with each drink it would only get uglier. She smoked two packs of cigarettes a day and more when she was drinking heavily. Joe would run down to the corner store and get her smokes even though he was too young.

I would try to stay out of her way but there were times that she wouldn't let me hide. She hit me many times as I grew up. I always got slapped in the face. Sometimes it was my fault because I said things that I shouldn't. She continually put me down and told me I was an ungrateful brat and would amount to nothing. I began to feel she was right. I spent a lot of time away from home because I just couldn't stand to be there. Many times I felt so guilty not being there to protect my little brother but I just didn't always have the energy to deal with her constant rages.

I liked school and made good grades in spite of her put downs. When I graduated from high school she was furious that I wanted to go to college but my father found a way for me to go. Though I didn't finish, because I met David, and he was going to Vietnam after he graduated from school. We wanted to get married right away. Fortunately, he didn't have to go to Nam. She was always mad about the money that I had wasted by not finishing school. If I had not gone to college I would not have met David. It was through a college friend that I met my husband. He was a good Christian man who introduced me to God and his grace.

My mother never let go of the fact that I wasted money and I never let go of the many times I had to drag her back from the local bar to help her get home. One time when I was fifteen I walked in the snow to bring her home. She pitched a fit but came with me. All the way home, she screamed and yelled at me but it didn't matter because I knew my brother Joe was so afraid that something would happen to her. We were afraid that she would freeze to death when she was out alone. Joe was younger than I, and he just wanted a mother. He loved her in spite of everything. I hated the fact that I couldn't protect him from her being his mother.

As Joe grew older she made him her drinking buddy. Misery loved company so she corrupted her own son. My little brother got into a lot of trouble with his drinking when he was in high school. It was hard for my father to see Joe self destruct. After Joe graduated from high school, he went into business with my father. My father had tried to help Joe with his addiction. We both knew that Joe didn't want to be the person he had become. Joe just didn't know how to change.

My mother was a very complex woman. We could never figure out what would set her off. Each day, she picked a new set of circumstances to get her upset.

I never had the greatest self-esteem, but after marrying David, that did improve. He would always tell me to try and put everything behind me and for the most part I did. It was a very painful childhood but I managed to separate myself from the past or so I thought. I am so lucky that I was not like my mother. I was always afraid I would be like her so I did everything possible so that I wouldn't. There were times I couldn't look into the mirror for fear of seeing her face in place of mine. I was wrapped up in how her drinking affected me that I didn't try to find out why she was who she was. I will never know because she died shortly after David died. It seems an eternity but it was only two years ago. I wish I could have helped my mother though I don't know what I could have done. If I had taken the time to ask, maybe it would have made a difference.

I took her in my home because she was dying of cancer. We talked about some things but I never asked her why she was so unhappy with me. Knowing my mother she didn't know why she drank, she just drank. At one time, she may have been able to pin point why but the years of drinking had clouded her mind and she didn't have an answer.

I told the congregation that my mother did say that she loved me in the end and that had made up for all of the times I hadn't heard it over the years. I even believed that she had found relief in the word of God because she would ask me to read the Bible to her. When I would read to her, I would detect a small smile on her face.

I realized that I was holding my reading glasses in my hand. I wasn't reading my message but speaking from the heart. God had moved into me and had helped me to tell my story. As I looked out, there were many tears, mine included. I had not allowed myself to cry about my mother. I never thought I was supposed to cry. I really thought if I didn't acknowledge what went on in my life, I could hide it from everyone. My father and brother and I never really talked about it. We were too afraid of how much it would hurt. I mentioned that Joe had found God over the past few years and was working with the youth at his local church. I was sure that they could since my pride in my baby brother.

I think many of the congregation had grown up with similar experiences and that's why they were so emotional. No one was judging me they were sympathizing and feeling my pain. I knew that I had to tell my story to those who needed to hear it. I was confident that this was not the only time I would be asked to share my words. I was sure that my experiences should be shared. It was as if the weight of the world had been lifted from my shoulders. I thanked God for my life, my family and my friends.

"God grant me the serenity to accept the
things I cannot change."

Chapter 22

More Than Just a Date

Dallas had become more than a friend. My Mercedes was keeping the highway hot from Pawley's to Atlanta. I was lucky to have found Dallas. He was one of the most caring men that I have ever met. When I was around him I would feel special again. To hold someone's hand and feel their connection is heart-warming. I was feeling as if I were in high school dating for the first time. I had forgotten just how sharing a conversation can make you feel. He laughs at my goofy jokes and I laugh at his. I mostly enjoyed the gentle way he kisses. I had forgotten how a little kiss could make me feel nervous with excitement. Dallas was so hurt by his divorce that he seemed to have his guard up sometimes, but little by little I could see it coming down.

His house was a beautiful old Atlanta home. I had seen homes like this in magazines but never up close and personal. He had hired a decorator to make it look like a perfect traditional home after he bought it. After he was divorced he looked for a house that made him feel comfortable. He told the decorator to make it look like a hunt club, and though it did, the house was still warm and inviting. It reminded me of the bed and breakfast David and I stayed when we traveled to Pinehurst, only prettier.

We traded off weekends. One weekend he would come to Pawley's, and the next weekend I would go to Atlanta. Dallas always asked me to bring Buddy. He was really getting close to Buddy. Everyone seemed to get close to Buddy easily. Buddy was my friend magnet.

When we were together, we didn't have to go anywhere. Spending time with each other was enough. We found pleasure sitting in front of a fire reading a good book. He loved law journals and I loved chick books. He read things to improve his mind and read things to improve my mood. Buddy just loved the fact that we were all together. I had missed the closeness of a companion for a long time, and loved this new feeling so much. We had grown so comfortable together that we didn't need words only human contact. Of course, eating played a giant part of our being together. Dallas had always planned his day around food. He was a man who loved good food and wine. I was beginning to gain a few pounds, but I needed a little more meat on my bones.

I wanted to ask him to go to Virginia with me over Christmas, but I was a little afraid that I might be rushing things. I didn't want to scare him off by introducing him to my four grandchildren. He didn't have any children of his own, so I didn't think he would want to spend a wild and crazy Christmas at our house.

I have always thought it sad that neither he nor Darrin had children. I had thought about asking him why neither one had children, but now was not the time. I hoped that he would volunteer the information on his own. It really didn't make any difference why he didn't have children, I was just curious.

I cannot imagine life without Michael and his family. I have needed them so much. You don't realize just how much you need your family until tragedy hits you. It is also nice to share happy times with people who really do care about you. I loved for the phone to ring and hear Lyle's voice on the other end. Lyle would call me a lot, usually, to tell me about something he had done or a good grade he had made. It always lifted my spirits to hear from him. He was missing me about as much as I was missing him.

I probably would ask Dallas if he wanted to come to Virginia anyway. What could it hurt? He could only say no and that would be fine too, though I would love to have the company. I had a feeling he would say yes, but I didn't want to get my hopes up.

After a few days had passed, I finally got up enough courage to ask Dallas to come with me to Virginia. I had decided to e-mail him, so that way if he said no, he couldn't see my disappointment. E-mail seemed a little impersonal but my ego was far too fragile to hear the word no.

Much to my surprise, he said yes. He was hoping all along that I would ask. He said that he had spent too many Christmases alone or as a pity guest of friends. He even wanted to take gifts to the children. He told me that he loved children but that his wife didn't want children because she didn't want to gain weight and not be able to loose it. She had been a beauty queen, Miss So-n-so something. Being beautiful was her main objective in life. He said she was never interested in anything that he wanted with the exception of his money and what it would buy. I had gotten my answer about children without having to ask. It is funny how things work that way. I was really glad to hear he liked children. Maybe he would change his mind after Christmas vacation. Things seemed so fast because I had only known him for about four weeks but it didn't seem that way.

My cottage was looking wonderful. Darrin was really creative. He had added so many little touches that I hadn't expected. His trim carpenter was unbelievable. Darrin had found an old barn, ready for demolition, and he bought all of the weathered wood. That beautiful old wood became the floors of my new addition. The old barn must have been a tobacco barn because I smelled a hint of tobacco as they were being installed. I had intricate molding everywhere. I am pretty sure that he gives me a special price because it would cost a fortune for someone else to build my little house. It is great to have good friends.

The temporary stairs to the turret were a little shaky but I still climbed up there to see the most incredible view. When I stand up there and feel the wind blow in my face it seems as if I could conquer the world. Maybe I shouldn't go so far as to say the world but maybe I could at least forget all the sadness that I endured over the past few years. It had been a long time since I had felt like a desirable woman. I liked that feeling. I felt full of joy. I had a stirring inside of me that I had longed for. Dallas had made me feel wonderful. He and David were somewhat alike in the way that they treated people. There were differences but both men were very special guys. I had been truly blessed twice. Both were southern gentlemen and knew how to make me feel special.

"Hello world."

Chapter 23

Merry Christmas, Hannah

We decided to take my car home for Christmas. Buddy fit better in my back seat. I wasn't sure Buddy would like being relegated to the rear but I was for sure not going to give him my seat. I was going to ride shotgun and Buddy was going to the back seat. Dallas had come to the Island a couple of days early to have my car checked over before we left. I was really impressed by his wanting to take care of me. I wasn't used to it but I liked it.

We had an incredibly fast trip. Dallas likes to drive straight through, with only one Buddy stop. As we got closer to Virginia, we noticed the mountains began to peek their little heads just above the horizon. As we drove closer they got bigger and bigger. When you could fully see the full view, the horizon had a deep blue hue. The Blue Ridge Mountains were as blue as I had remembered, but I saw them in a completely different light. I had been looking at them through tears for the past few years and now I could see them clearly.

I felt such excitement. I couldn't wait for the family to meet Dallas and I couldn't wait for Dallas to meet them. I wondered if Lyle would like him. Lyle was not someone who would share his grandmother willingly. His reaction was really important to me. What if he hated Dallas? I thought about that, but realized that it might take time for him to adjust to his grandmother having another man in her life.

As we got closer to home, that old familiar home sweet home feeling warmed me inside. Dallas seemed a little quiet. I asked him if he was ready for this and he chuckled and answered me in a funny way. He told me he felt like he was on a first date and going to meet my father. He said he always felt uncomfortable in that situation. Dallas said when he was growing up he would find himself stumbling for words when he got nervous. I asked him if he was nervous about meeting Michael. He laughed and said, no he was nervous about meeting the children. He was hopeful that they would like him. I thought it was funny that he and I were worried about the same thing. I told him that it didn't matter what anyone thought but me. He grabbed my hand and smiled. Then I told him Buddy liked him so Lyle would like him as well.

When we arrived, Mary Lee had dinner ready. I hated that we wouldn't have time to sit and talk before we converged around the dinner table on top of each other. Dallas seemed very at quiet during dinner. Lyle and Sarah seemed to be sizing him up. They stared at Dallas so much that I was afraid he was a little uncomfortable. He kept wiping his face with his napkin. He must have thought he had food on his face the way the children were staring at him. Everything was going too well. Sissy started telling me about school and in the same breath, without missing a beat, asked if Dallas and I were going to get married. I nearly choked and found myself at a loss for words. Dallas and I had never mentioned that word. We were still getting to know each other.

Dallas smiled and looked at me and said, "Are we going to get married?"

I found myself totally speechless, even stunned. Finally, I looked at him and said with a smile, "I haven't thought about that. Mr. DuPuy and I are just friends, really good friends."

That seemed to satisfy everyone. Dallas even looked relieved. I think he wanted to put the ball in my court and see where I stood, since things were moving so fast.

As fond of him as I was, I wasn't ready to think about marriage. I hadn't even thought anything further than what we already have. I was enjoying this new relationship just as it was unfolding. I was a little afraid that I might loose his friendship if I thought about marriage. If I were to get married again, he would be a good candidate. We were both comfortable with each other. Dallas and I had been married and our hearts were scarred. We were still in a healing process. Four weeks is not enough time to think about marriage, though I think that was about the length of time David and I started talking about marriage.

After dinner, Dallas asked Michael to help him clean the kitchen. Mary Lee was smiling from ear to ear but Michael wasn't smiling. In fact, he was frowning. Dallas knew that I loved spending time with Mary Lee. We needed to have girl talk and this was a perfect time. Mary Lee was curious to know how I felt about Dallas. I wasn't exactly sure, but I knew I wanted him in my life.

When it was time for bed, I kissed Dallas goodnight as he left for the garage apartment. I was glad to hear that the air conditioner and the heat had been replaced. The apartment was now suited for year round habitation.

For the next few days, we shopped and shopped. Dallas wasn't used to shopping in such a small town, but he said that he thought it was perfect for him. The word he kept saying was quaint. He loved the area because everything anyone could want was all within a square block. He found a coffee shop that we frequented during our visit. Mary Lee didn't make good coffee and Dallas was rather grumpy and gruff until he had finished his first cup of strong coffee. I wasn't a coffee drinker but a tea drinker. I found some really interesting teas to enjoy each morning. It was really nice to have someone fix my breakfast and clean up after me.

Christmas Eve came and we headed off to church. The children were in the program so we left early to get a front row seat. We had forgotten that there were other children in the program so all of the front row seats were gone. That was for the better because baby David talked through the entire program. When he saw Lyle, he began to squeal with great excitement. Lyle got so flustered that he forgot all of his lines. He was embarrassed but stayed on stage like a trooper. Once the program was over, he was fine. He was ready to go home and play video games. It doesn't take much to keep him happy.

After church, we rode around the city to see the beautiful lights. We always went to this one house that was a grand display of lights and the Christmas Spirit. The owner of the house must start in October to get it all finished. He received a unanimous vote from the Fry car as the best of the evening. Even when the lights are a little tacky, they still prove that Christmas is alive.

When we got home, it was time for the children to climb into bed. After Michael read "The Night before Christmas," they kissed us all goodnight and tip toed up to bed. It wasn't more than two minutes when Lyle came down and sat between Dallas and me. He wanted to tell us that he no longer believed in Santa Clause. He said that he had to pretend that he believed because of the other children. Lyle said that big brothers had to keep the secret. Looking at him I wondered just how long he could keep this "really" big secret.

Christmas morning came very early. I think we no sooner had put out the toys that the children were up and running around. Much to my surprise, when I went into the kitchen there sat Dallas drinking instant coffee with my tea steeping and ready to drink. He said he didn't want to miss a minute of the chaos.

Buddy was beside himself. He had not seen so much action since the children had been in Pawley's last June. He ran around in circles for about ten minutes. Finally, he settled into one spot as the rest of the crew ran around in circles. First, Buddy chased his tail and then the children chased each other. It exhausted me just watching.

Packages were opened and paper was flying. If this didn't scare Dallas off, nothing was going to. He sat back in his chair with his arms across his chest just smiling. I went over and sat on the arm of his chair and asked why he was smiling and he shook his head and said, "All these years, I've wanted this, and now that I have it, I know that I missed a lot. Call me crazy, but this is fun".

I hugged his head as if he were a child. I felt something when I hugged him that I had never felt before. I knew that Dallas was more than a really good friend. I was afraid of what I was feeling, but I felt he was feeling the same thing.

Later that morning, when everything had settled down we went into the living room to exchange our gifts. I had found an old picture of his home place in his office on one of my visits to Atlanta. I had swiped it from his desk. I felt a little guilty, but I wanted to do something special and thoughtful. I knew how important his childhood was and this would be just a small reminder. It surprised me that he hadn't missed it. If he did miss it he never mentioned it. Knowing Dallas, he would have thought his cleaning lady had moved it and forgotten to replace it in the original position.

I had taken it to a local artist at home and had her paint an oil painting of it. She had done such an incredible rendition of the picture. I had shown it to Darrin and he was jealous. Carrie asked if I cared if she did the same thing and of course, I said no. Deep down I really didn't want her to copy me but what could I say? They kept the secret because when I showed Dallas the picture, he was stunned and emotional. He was truly moved by my gift. It was such a change in what I had felt last Christmas. Last Christmas was such a low point in my life.

Then he said it was his turn to give me my gift. I had no idea what he could have gotten me. He left the room and then walked in with a really big box. He didn't have the box in the car and he hadn't been shopping without me, so where in the world did the box come from. What in the world could be in the box? I was like the children ripping the paper off. I opened the first box and there was another box wrapped just like the larger one and then there was another and another. This was the work of Mary Lee. I finally got to a box which was the size of a small jewelry box. It wasn't a ring box because it was flatter. When I opened it, I saw a beautiful diamond heart pendent. There were two small but beautiful hearts entwined. It sparkled brilliantly. Then Dallas said, "These hearts are ours. They are entwined as we are and they sparkle like the stars that I see when I look into your eyes. I love you Hanna Fry. I know that you are not ready for marriage, but I want you to know that I will be here when you are ready."

All I could do was hug him. His words had taken me by surprise. I wanted to tell him that I loved him but I wasn't ready. Dallas put his arm around me and said, "I know that this is soon, but I have waited for a very long time for someone like you to be in my life. I will be here when you are ready to say the words. I know that you care deeply for me and in time, you will love me as I do you." I smiled and said, "Be patient Mr. DuPuy. This is all new to me."

When night fall came and we all had eaten too much, we retired to our beds early. When I got into bed I said my prayers as usual but this time my prayers took much longer. I thanked God for the perfect day, then I thanked Him for all of my experiences. Everything that had happened in my life came running through my mind that night. My mind was mixed with good and bad times but my reaction was much more accepting than before. Maybe I had changed or maybe I had finally come to terms with who I am. I used to cry about my life. Sometimes I would cry until I would double over in grief. I always thought that I had been cheated somehow. Cheated because someone, somewhere had a better life than I. I wanted that vine covered cottage with only love and happiness on the inside. I thought that was what life was all about. When I dreamed about my life it would be like a scene from a movie with the theme from "Terms of Endearment."

I grew older, probably not wiser, but more experienced. I know now that tears only dampen the circumstances. I learned that with love, you don't always have happiness. There are going to be bad times. That vine covered cottage will get dusty and dirty. You just have to open your eyes and see the problem and clean up your mess. Finally, you praise God for not letting you live a boring, perfect life. We all have to have heavy hearts at some point in our lives but we turn our eyes to Jesus and let his big heart beat for our broken one.

As sleep overcame me, I felt as if my heart would explode with love. My heart was full of my memories. Though some are sad they are my memories. My memories will always be with me and no one can take them away. These are the memories of my heart.

"And I think to myself, what a wonderful world."
-Louis Armstrong

Chapter 24

Ahead of the Storm

Two Days after Christmas, Dallas, Buddy and I headed back to South Carolina because of a giant snow storm prediction. We enjoyed our visit so much and would have like to have stayed longer but I think that my father was right when he would tell us that house guests and fish start to smell after they are around too long.

We had an uneventful trip home. When we arrived at the cottage, the lights were on and Carrie and Darrin were waiting for us. They were so glad to see us and told us over and over how much they had missed us. Cuddles was pretty happy to see Buddy, also. They ran around the house for about an hour, until they both collapsed, with their tongues hanging out.

Darrin ordered his usual five pizzas though we never finish more than two. He just can't make a decision, so he orders one with pepperoni, two veggie pizzas with and without onions and of course, a meat lover's calorie feast but the winning choice is always the Hawaiian pizza with pineapple and ham. The first time he ordered it I thought

145

he was crazy but now it's my favorite. We all fight over the last piece.

The addition to the cottage is about finished and looks spectacular. I think my favorite part is the turret. When you climb to the top you feel as if you are on top of the world and almost in the clouds. At night, the stars are so close you can almost reach out and touch them. It's like a little piece of Heaven right here on Pawley's Island. I am feeling a little overindulgent but that never stopped me before. Besides, the children will love this place even more and want to spend their summers with their old granny.

We had all decided not to do anything for New Years except stay at home and enjoy each others company. Dallas was going to go back to Atlanta the next morning because he had been away for two weeks and needed to be in court for a hearing toward the end of the week. I hated that he had to go back because we had such a wonderful holiday and I didn't want to see it come to an end.

We have not talked about the fact that he had told me he loved me Christmas night or that I didn't tell him I loved him. I knew that I owed him an explanation before he returned to Atlanta. Though he had said that he would wait for me, I didn't want to risk losing him by not explaining myself. I had no real explanation to give him. It just didn't come out of my mouth. I had only said those words to David and I just had to be sure before I said the words to Dallas. I would hate to say I love you and find out that I'm feeling something else.

I am pretty sure what I am feeling is love. One thing I am positive about is that I know I want him in my life. I can't picture the future without him, but saying I love you isn't easy for me. Maybe what I'm feeling is fear of losing him. I don't know what it is, I just know that I like the way things are between us now and I don't want that to change and I was so afraid that it would.

It had been unusually warm for New Year's in Pawley's. We all took the dogs on the beach for a long walk. Actually, the dogs took us for a run. I just couldn't believe how beautiful the beach looked at that time of the year. There are no tourists and very few people on the Island. Most of the locals had gone out of town and hadn't returned from the holidays. Carrie, Darrin and Dallas had come to stay the night. We were all going to try to stay up and watch the ball drop but we all knew that would be a fight to the end. We had a bet of sorts going as to who would crash first. The first person asleep had to fix breakfast and clean the kitchen. I was pretty sure that it would be me but I was going to fight hard not to fall asleep.

Dallas and I went for a walk after supper. I knew he wanted to talk and I was so afraid of what I would say. As we walked he grabbed for my hand. It felt so nice to have my hand held. The little things were what I had missed the most after David died. As we walked, Dallas talked about everything but what I thought was on his mind. He told me that he was going to miss me when he went back to Atlanta and wanted me to come to visit after he was finished with the upcoming court hearing.

I was so relieved. I just knew that he wanted to know why I hadn't replied when he told me that he loved me but he never brought it up. What a fun night we all had and, as predicted, I was the first to fall asleep. Breakfast was great and the kitchen was spotless. I failed to mention that I didn't clean the kitchen alone because Dallas felt guilty and helped me. I think they all fell asleep shortly after my eyes had succumbed to the powers of tiredness.

It was time for Dallas to return to Atlanta. I was pretty sad, but knowing that I was going there in about two weeks made it bearable. He kissed me goodbye and pulled out of the driveway. No sooner did he pull out he turned around and said "Hannah, I'm still waiting and I will for as long as it takes." Dallas smiled and backed out of the driveway and tooted the horn. I knew he loved me and I was happy knowing that someone loved me again.

I couldn't help but laugh because this time he didn't give me a chance to respond. It popped in my head to say I love you but it didn't come out of my mouth.

At the end of the week, Darrin and Carrie called to tell me they had some great news to share. The first thing that came to mind was they were getting another dog because I knew at their age they couldn't be pregnant. They assured me that wasn't their news.

We went out to dinner and Darrin ordered champagne. He raised his glass and said he wanted to toast his new neighbor. I was puzzled but so stunned that I just sat and shrugged my shoulders.

Come to find out, Darrin had been looking for the right piece of property on the Island for about a year. He said that when he started work on my place he felt closeness to the area. He loved the quaintness of Pawley's and the history it exuded. The Island just had a feeling or maybe it was a life of its own. Darrin felt as if he was drawn to Pawley's as if there were a connection through his spirit.

Finally, I got around to asking him what property he bought. He laughed so hard that when he said, "Hannah when I said neighbors, I meant next door neighbors." I hardly could understand what he was saying because he was laughing so hard. When I finally got it through my hollow skull I was so excited I squealed with delight. Everyone in the restaurant looked at me as if I was crazy, but I didn't care. I turned and lifted my glass of champagne and toasted everyone around me. After a few minutes, I got around to asking him how in the world he managed to buy Ruth and Bobby's house. Darrin said that he was doing a job for Emil Tasco, the partner of the guy who had bought the house. His partner mentioned that they wanted to sell some of their properties because the economy was so bad that they didn't think that there would be too many vacationers for the next few years. Also, with interest rates and gas prices mounting so high, they were going to unload a few houses. When Darrin asked about the house next door to me, he said that wasn't one of the properties they wanted to sell but he would ask his partner. Darrin told him to call if he ever decided to sell it. He called him a couple of days ago and Darrin didn't even ask Carrie because he knew how happy she would be to live next door to me.

Happy was a complete understatement. We were both ecstatic. Carrie finally got a chance to talk and didn't stop for about thirty minutes. She had it all planned out to the point she knew what she wanted to put on her front porch. Darrin said the move wouldn't take long because they were going to rent their house to a school teacher moving into the area in the spring. Her husband was already here and renting an apartment but she really wanted a house with an option to buy and Darrin thought that would be perfect for all parties involved.

After a number of weeks passed, slowly but surely, the DuPuy's moved into their house. Carrie painted the house a soft yellow with white trim and a green front door. Not a bright green but a beautiful Charleston Green. It was so different from the weathered blue that Ruth had on the house though the blue fit Bobby and Ruth. It was a much happier look especially after all that had happened. I was so happy to see the change and I was sure that Ruth would have approved.

Darrin had already decided to put in a pool so the yard had been demolished. He reassured everyone that it would be beautiful when he finished, but he had a long way to go.

When Darrin and Carrie completed their overhaul of the house, it would have nothing left of Ruth. I found that a little sad but I understood why Carrie was changing the house from Ruth's house to hers and I was glad that the changes took away the reminder of the last memories of Ruth's illness.

Dallas and I had been back and forth a lot from Atlanta to Pawley's and keeping the highway hot. His court hearing lasted a little longer than he had thought but I still went for weekends to visit. I looked forward to seeing him more and more. We were having a great time together and I hadn't thought about much of anything but our relationship and where all of this would lead. I just wanted to live for the present. I knew that I loved him but had not told him just yet. I was going to find the right time because I wanted it to be special. I had been relying on God for everything else in my life and I was going to let Him direct me.

June was right around the corner and my addition was finished. It was just waiting for the family to come after school was out. I was so excited for them to come and spend time with me. I had missed them so much. I hadn't been to Virginia since December and that's a long time.

Carrie and Darrin were in the house next door. It was really beautiful and Darrin was right about the yard. It looked like a magazine cover. I loved the fence he had installed around the pool. Not only was the Carolina jasmine spectacular running along the fence as if it had always been there vining along the pickets, but with the children coming to visit it was a much needed safety feature.

Baby David was not only walking, he was running and climbing like a little monkey.

It was hard to believe that when they started, the house looked like a dark weathered beach cottage and now it was a bright low country show place. The siding had been changed from horizontal to vertical. Just that change made the house look taller and more impressive. Darrin had put on a new porch which wrapped completely around the house. I do think that my favorite part was the landscaping. It was clean and colorful. I could not have dreamed anything better.

"The stone that the builders rejected has now become the corner stone."
-Psalm 118:22, the Living Bible

Chapter 25

Moving Forward

When the children arrived, the first thing they wanted to do was go to the ocean. They stripped off their clothes and threw on their suits and bolted. On the way, they spied the pool next door. Needless to say, we never got to the ocean because the pool was just too tempting and, as the children told me, there were no sharks! The girls were so happy that they didn't have to get sand in their bathing suits. As all females know, it never fails that you always get sand in the crotch of your suit. It is one very uncomfortable experience that lasts far beyond the minute you discover the sand has irritated everything it touched. I must say that a real perk for having a swimming pool right next door, is the absence of sand.

Much to my surprise, they arrived with a new addition to the family. Lyle had gotten a dog for his twelfth birthday. He wasn't turning twelve until September but he fell in love with a yellow lab puppy one of his friends had. He drove Mary Lee crazy about getting a dog and she caved after seeing the puppy. Of course, he made all the promises about taking complete care of the dog and they believed him. Sumo was adorable but Buddy was a little unsure of him. I figured they would soon bond and become fast friends. Buddy usually warms up fast to most dogs, both big and small.

The cottage came alive with dogs and children. This old house had just been waiting for someone to come along and love it. If a house can have a personality, this one certainly does. It reminds me of an old pair of jeans perfectly broken in and shabby in all of the right places. I was drawn to it the first time I saw it and this old cottage will be a part of me from now on.

Michael would only be staying for a few days so he wanted to relax as much as he could with so many of us in the house. I felt sorry for him because he didn't seem to find any peace while he was here. Hopefully, he could rest while he was back in Virginia and the family stayed with me. The quiet would probably drive him crazy.

Every time the baby would get to sleep, someone would come in and bang the screen door and wake him up. We finally got smart and locked the doors so the children would have to knock.

Dallas came in for the weekend before Michael had to leave. He had bought a boat and wanted to take Michael out on the water with him. Dallas, Darrin and Michael enjoyed their guy time together. I know that Michael doesn't look at Dallas as a replacement for his father but he does like him a lot. They took Lyle out for a ride but he wanted to come back because he was having withdrawals from his video games.

The girls and I went shopping almost everyday. They loved the outlets, and so did I because of the low prices… since I was footing the bill. We bought lots of cute sundresses for them and of course, we had to have matching flip flops and hair accessories. I had so much fun spoiling them and I think they had a lot of fun letting me spoil them.

Three weeks passed much too quickly and all of a sudden they were packing things to leave. It was sad for me because I enjoyed their visit so much. Though a little of me was ready to have some quiet-time.

We were all going to go to Darrin's and Carrie's for a farewell cookout. Dallas and I had gone to the market to buy crab and shrimp. We were going to have a huge seafood feast to say good bye. Dallas was going to make Frogmore stew. The children thought it sounded so silly but they were disappointed when they found out that there were no frogs in it. And of course, Darrin would wear his "World's Greatest Cook" apron while manning the grill.

While we were out Dallas took me by to see a condo on The Island. I was thinking that he wanted to buy it for investment purposes but he said he was going to move to Pawley's right away.

I was so confused because I thought he would never leave Atlanta and his beautiful home. Dallas said he was ready to retire and spend time fishing and helping Darrin start a new building project. I was shocked, thrilled...all at the same time. In the past, when Dallas would leave to go home, I would miss him before he had left the city limits. Now, he will say goodnight and I will get to see him the next day. I was so excited that he was going to be so close.

Our seafood feast was really a pig out. We had corn on the cob, potato salad, green beans, filet, shrimp, crab, gallons of sweet tea and hot dogs because the little kids and the big kids wanted hot dogs. The men must have eaten three hot dogs a piece and that was only hors d'oeuvres. I am pretty sure our arteries were screaming for Lipitor or at least oatmeal to wash away the plaque.

Morning came too fast and the van pulled away. The girls were blowing kisses and just as they pulled out of the driveway, they rolled the windows down and screamed out "We love you Grandma!" I knew I would miss them but I knew another adventure was about to begin.

"You must be this tall to ride this ride."

Chapter 26

Arrival

I have had a wonderful summer though I always think that summer goes by much too fast. Summer is a feeling. It's really hard to put into words. When I was in school I would get so excited about sleeping late and soaking up the warm rays. It was knowing that you were free for a few months with no tests to be taken, no real schedule to be followed and a feeling of fun every day. This past summer had much of that feeling and it's because of Dallas.

The condo that Dallas bought needed a lot of work, but the views make up for everything that it lacks. The master bedroom overlooks the marsh and has a balcony with a new canvas awning covering it. It is beautiful but the bugs try to eat you alive, so using the balcony is a real challenge. He uses the second bedroom as an office. He completely has redone most of the place to fit his needs and it's almost as beautiful as his place in Atlanta now that the renovation is finished.

Dallas is such a kind and thoughtful man. My feelings for him have become way more than just friendship. I'm sure his moving here has been what has changed everything. Or maybe it has just opened my eyes to see that we need to be together forever.

When I am alone and have my talks with God, I ask Him why I should be so lucky to have had two wonderful men love me. I almost feel guilty because I have been so blessed.

David was such a rock and motivator in my life. His passion for others was a beacon of light for me to follow. I learned so much from his example. He taught me to care about others with a great intensity. David was completely unselfish and generous and I diligently try to follow his example; though more often than not, I fall short.

Dallas is a lot like David but he is, if it's possible, even more generous. He not only gives money, but much of his time to anyone who may need him. Since he is partially retired, he finds time to help build homes for the poor on Saturdays with Darrin. The two DuPuy boys are well known for their building expertise and kindness. They usually supply their time and money building comfortable homes for those who can't otherwise have a home. I have no idea how much money the boys spend and I don't really want to know. I just know that they are earning their stars in Heaven.

Fall is now pushing summer on its way. I will miss the summer but fall is such a calm and peaceful time of the year.

One week ago, Dallas asked me again to marry him. For the first time in a long time, I didn't stumble or have the slightest hesitation in my voice. I looked at him and said yes. I wasn't afraid anymore to fall in love and for everyone to know that I was in love with Dallas. I think I have been so afraid to open this door and walk through.

Waiting has been very hard for Dallas, so we have decided to have the ceremony soon. Carrie and Darrin want to have it around the pool, so we are going to be married the first week in October. Our families will be our guests, along with our baby, Buddy. I cannot wait to be married to such a wonderful man.

Carrie is making a bit of a fuss about things, but since she is doing much of the work, I'm letting her take the bull by the horns and tackle him. Her love of flowers will be obvious, I'm sure. The pool will be decked out in foliage. I doubt there will be a flower available from Pawley's to Charleston.

Darrin and Dallas want to have a barbeque, and that sounds great to me. I had a wedding once before and I am not a spring chicken, so I will go with the flow. The only thing that I am worried about is getting barbeque sauce on my dress, but maybe we can get some lobster bibs. I wonder if they make a wedding addition of the lobster bibs for messy brides.

Lyle is really excited about getting a new granddaddy. I think that the girls are happy too but they are a little worried about sharing their granny. Baby David will be happy to just be here and run with all of the dogs. This will really be like a family reunion for all of us. Joe and Sherry will be here with their adopted girls.

They call them their own but they are really foster children. Now that they are fifteen, I don't think that they will be going anywhere. They are family as far as anyone is concerned and always will be.

Dallas and Darrin have an uncle who is ninety-two and he will be coming. Uncle Bo is Dallas' mother's brother and the last of the clan on that side of the family. I think this is adding up to be a real circus but it sounds perfect to me. I understand that Uncle Bo can't hear and he doesn't see well either, but he does like the women. He was married three times that the boys know about, but they think that there could be a few more around somewhere.

I have so many memories of David and they are a part of me forever and now I will add to the memory book of my heart with Dallas. I have learned to appreciate each day with excitement and respect. You never know when your time on this beautiful earth will be over, so with each and every breath, I think God for all that I had and all that is ahead of me.

October has arrived and the time has come for me to walk down the aisle and take the hand of my new husband. I am so proud to be his wife and I think that he is just as proud to be my husband. The sky is glorious and the weather is perfect. This day is what every bride dreams about.

We are together with our family and friends sharing such a special time in our lives together. My mind is racing all over the place and my heart is pounding but when I get a glimpse of Dallas a calm comes over me. As I walk towards him I pick up the pace because I can't wait to get there. He reaches out to take my hand and smiles. We almost laugh out loud. The minister talks but I do not hear a word all I hear is when he says that Dallas can kiss me and he does. Mr. and Mrs. Dallas Walker DuPuy walk hand in hand down the aisle, now married.

The barbeque has been so much fun. We have eaten way too much and have danced even more. We are taking a limo to the airport to fly to Florida so that tomorrow we can fly to Barbados.

Barbados has lived up to the pictures in the brochures. It is everything they promised and more. We have had such a fun, relaxed time; not much different from being at home. I have to pinch myself over and over to make sure this is not a dream because it really feels like a fantasy being married to Dallas. We will be going back home in a few days and settle into our new life.

We have decided to live in my cottage, our cottage, and rent Dallas' condo, which shouldn't be hard after all of the work he put into it. I know that Buddy will be beside himself when we get home. He will be slobbering all over us and we will be happy to see his slobber.

As I think about all that has happened in my life, I feel such happiness. I think of my mother and I do find that I wish I could have said that I was sorry for having held on to such resentment for so long, but I think she knows. I think of my daddy and say thank you for loving me so much. I remember Joe always being there for everyone. I also thank God for my son Michael for being so strong. When I think of David I always smile because he was such a source of happiness for me. Now I look into Dallas' eyes and I feel so safe, secure and loved. I am truly a lucky woman. Our life together will be a new adventure and I am looking forward to every minute. My heart is full of beautiful memories and I know it has room for many more. When I pass from this earth, I know that I will go to Heaven and there I will tell all who will listen about the memories of my heart.

Biography

Beth lives in Southwest Virginia with her husband of forty years. She has four children, Holland, Maggie, Wilson and Byron. Beth is the second, of four girls. Her love of John Steinbeck sparked her interest in writing when she was fifteen. She attributes her vivid imagination to her life experiences.